ESCAPE TO THE SKIES

ESCAPE TO THE SKIES

DAVE JOHNSON

Copyright © 2024 Dave Johnson. All rights reserved

Escape to the Skies is a work of fiction. Any references to historical events, real people, or real places are used fictitiously. Other names, characters, places and events are products of the author's imagination and any resemblance to actual events, places or persons, living or dead, is entirely coincidental.

No part of this book may be reproduced, or stored in a retrieval system, or transmitted in any form or by any means, electronic, mechanical, photocopying, recording, or otherwise, without express written permission of the publisher.

Cover art by Creative Covers
ISBN: 9781739132699

To all the my relatives.

Whether you are in the UK, the US, Canada, Jamaica, France or Australia (naming some of the places we have scattered to), the airship "Rebel" is coming your way.

The Rebel Runaway Series

1, Freedom Skies.

2, Troubled Skies.

3, Escape to the Skies.

The Stuck Series

1, Stuck in Time.

2, Stuck 1595: An Elizabethan Adventure.

3, Stuck 1824: A London Tale.

4, Stuck 1855: Lucy Travels East.

5, Stuck 1966: No Time To Groove.

6, Stuck in the Land of the Pharaohs.

7, Stuck Between Two Lives.

All "Stuck" books are stand-alone stories

CHAPTER ONE

'Sometimes, I wonder why I'm even doing this,' ruminated Charlotte, 'It's risky and reckless. But then again, I had a pretty safe and comfortable life in the days before I joined the Rebel Runaways, and it was deadly boring, so what the hell!' Glancing over her shoulder, she called out to Billy, who was lying on the airship's deck, peering through the open doorway. 'How's it looking?'

'Dahn a bit. Oops! Too bloomin' much! Up a touch. Perfick! Keep 'er there.'

Below, suspended by a harness on the end of a rope, Jake was armed with nothing more than a brush and a pot of paint. The airship, The Rebel, had ventured deep into enemy territory and was hovering above the Air-Fleet airfield. Tethered below were thirteen airships bristling with weapons, glistening in the moonlight. Joshua and Sadie stood vigilant on lookout duty. Joshua was wearing his Gauntlet, which could fire a harpoon from a great distance, powered by a clockwork motor. Sadie, meanwhile wore her dart-firing Glove. They hoped they would not have to use them, as any confrontation, even if they emerged from it unscathed, would signal a failure of their mission.

'Ee's finished that 'un,' shouted Billy, 'On ter the next, bleedin' pronto!'

The following morning: the day of the Air-Fleet fly-past, Green Park, London.

The top brass were awaiting the arrival of the airships. Previously, Members of Parliament would have joined them, but now that the armed forces had taken over the Government, all the politicians were at home, sulking.

'It's been a splendid day so far,' remarked General Truscott, 'Even the cavalry looked a fine fighting force, bearing in mind there are no horses left alive.'

'Yes, and the crowds are something to behold. There are three times more than I would have expected. The park is almost bursting at the seams!' replied the country's leader, Field Marshal Bellings.

'Just a simple fly-past in formation, and that will be that. We can call the day a resounding success. What could go wrong? The Air-Fleet pilots might not be able to march in step like proper soldiers, but surely they can fly in a line!' said Truscott, somewhat tetchily.

In the midst of the crowd, Jed was puzzled.

'Ere, wot's everyone wavin' them booklets for?' he

asked the man beside him.

'It's 'cause of the lottery,' came the reply from Seth.

'What lottery?' asked Jed.

'Where you bin? On the moon or summat? Surely you knows about the Sky Blue Lottery? Well, you're too late to enter now. It was in one of them pamphlets, with a Rebel Runaways story. All you 'ad to do was pay a penny to one of the Sky Blue charity ladies and do an anagram of Rebel Runaways.'

'Wots a anger-ram?'

'It's when you arrange the letters in a different order, only in this case it don't have to make another word. The answer is going to be revealed by the Air-Fleet.'

'A penny ain't much.'

'Exactly, no skill needed; it's just luck. Someone could be very rich and win half of all them pennies. There's a lot of folks entered - more than the people you can see waving their booklets.'

'Oh, no! Bleedin'' ell. I missed out! So what's 'appening to the other half then?'

'Charity. It's all going to the Puffin' Billy Soup Station. One of the Runaways, not surprisingly called Billy, is setting up soup kitchens to feed street urchins.'

'How will you know if you've won?'

'No idea. Just got to wait for the airships. I'm surprised the Air-Fleet are playin' ball. I thought them and the Runaways was enemies!'

High up above the park, hidden in the clouds, The Rebel Runaways were also awaiting the arrival of the Air-Fleet.

'What do we do if no one gets the letters in the right order,' asked Charlotte.

'Then we keep all the money,' replied Jake, who had

devised the idea. It said quite clearly in the rules that the winner had to get all the letters in the right order. It's not as easy as you might think. There are over eight thousand different combinations of thirteen letters. I found quite a few proper anagrams - "Beryl unawares", for instance.'

'Who's Beryl?' asked Sadie.

'Dunno!' chipped in Billy with a grin, 'I don't fink she knows either; she's unaware!'

'And there's "uneasy brawler",' continued Jake.

'That's coz he knows the Rebel Runaways are on the case,' laughed Billy.

'Swear urbanely,' suggested Jake.

'What does urbanely mean?' asked Genevieve.

'It means you are well-mannered, relaxed and confident,' explained Charlotte.

'Rather like me,' added Oliver.

'Stone the crows! Swear urbanely?' scoffed Billy, 'I'm bleedin' confident about swearin' all the bloomin' time.'

Charlotte took the Rebel down so they could peer through the clouds.

'Cor blimey, take a butcher's. 'Ere they come!' yelled Billy.

'Do you think they will have spotted what we were up to last night?' asked Charlotte, worried that their careful planning would all have been for nothing.

'I would be extremely surprised,' replied Jake. 'I was very neat, and I mixed them all up. I doubt they would have noticed, and if they did, they would presume it was an official demarcation.'

'When they are directly below us, Charlotte,' said Oliver, 'Take her down as low as you dare. The Air-Fleet won't be looking up. Most of them won't be able to see us anyway; just those at the back might spot us, but I doubt it.

Even then, they won't know whether to break ranks and chase us or stay in position for the parade. Once we've said hello, you can take her up again, and we'll be away to Paris. They won't think of looking for us there!'

On the ground, the crowd was expectant.

'Here, they are!' shouted Seth to Jed, cheering enthusiastically and waving his booklet. 'I've got my letters written on the front of this.'

'So what you lookin' for?' asked Jed.

'I dunno. Oh, look. Painted on the back of the airship in red is the letter A. That's my first letter. Then the next one has got an N. I've got that too!' As each airship flew past, Seth ticked off the letters on the back, getting more and more excited with each one.

'That's it,' he yelled finally, jumping up and down, 'It's me! They spell "Any Warbler Sue", I've won!'

'Who's Sue?'

'It's my wife's name.'

'Well, she's certainly got something to sing about now!'

The noise from the rest of the crowd had not abated. Even though the spectators knew they hadn't won, they were thrilled to be part of the occasion. Their mood was lifted to a state of hysteria by the sight of the Rebel Runaways waving from the gondola's open door only twenty feet above the Air-Fleet.

Bellings was completely oblivious to the situation. He didn't know about the lottery and didn't realise the red letters on each airship were a recent addition. He waved magnanimously at the crowd, mistakenly accepting their praise and gratitude. He first realised something was amiss when he saw the Rebel descend from the clouds and hover tantalisingly above the Air-Fleet. Like the rest of his cabinet, he pointed furiously at the enemy airship to no effect. In the leading Air-Fleet ship, Wing Commander Curbishly was at the helm.

'It's going rather well, don't you think?' he said smugly. 'That's what I call a warm welcome. I think the reputation of the Air-Fleet will have risen in Field Marshal Bellings' eyes.' If he had looked out of his gondola's rear window, he might just have caught sight of the Rebel soaring up into the clouds, but he didn't. He was too busy patting himself on the back.

Later that day, after they had returned to the airfield, one of the aircrew ran up to Curbishly, saluted and handed him a booklet.

'Sir, I think you ought to see this.' Curbishly read the information about the lottery, then strode over to where the airships were tethered. It took him a while to spot the red letters painted on each of them.

'Corporal! Get these letters painted over. I don't want a word of this to get back to Field Marshal Bellings. Do you understand me?'

'So, wot we doing in Paris, then?' asked Billy.

'Just a flying visit, so to speak,' laughed Oliver. 'We have a building to inspect before we sign the lease in Rue du Faubourg Saint-Honoré.'

'Holy mackerel, that's a bloomin' mouthful! Roo du fourber santa nory. Why can't they 'ave proper names like The Old Kent Road?'

'It's going to be a great address for our fashion house,' enthused Genevieve.

'We'll have to make a quick decision,' replied Oliver, 'There's some up-and-coming design house called Hermès after it. Then, after that, I suggest a glass of champagne in Saint-Germain-des-Prés to celebrate our lottery success.'

'Ere we go again!' remarked Billy, 'San German de pray! Wot's than then, a bleedin' church wot sells German sausages?'

'No,' laughed Oliver, 'It's an exclusive area for wining and dining.'

'Cor blimey, so we're gettin' blotto on the lotto!'

DAVE JOHNSON

CHAPTER TWO

As he strolled across Westminster Bridge, Joshua adjusted the new necktie he had purchased on the Rebel's recent trip to Paris . He rarely walked that way into the West End because there were always so many soldiers in the area, and he found it hard to be inconspicuous. Tall and well-built, Joshua towered over most Londoners he encountered. Admittedly, he wouldn't look so tall if he wasn't wearing his favourite top hat, the one decorated with brass cogs. Then again, he might blend in if he hadn't chosen to wear his tartan cape. The fact that he was black and dressed like a member of the upper classes set him apart. While there were other black individuals in London, most were to be found labouring on the docks or working as domestic servants. None, however would saunter confidently across the bridge with as much self-belief as Joshua, ex-slave and proud member of the Rebel Runaways. If he had been scurrying along, darting furtively between the shadows, he might have attracted attention from the bored young men guarding the Houses of Parliament. However, Joshua was demonstrating the art of hiding in plain sight, and his progress went unnoticed.

As he passed a black woman heading in the opposite direction, Joshua touched the brim of his hat in greeting. It was a small gesture of politeness, but he always did this when meeting people of colour and hoped it would convey the message that he considered them to be important. The woman, who looked like a servant by her attire, stopped and stared at Joshua, open-mouthed with astonishment. He smiled and continued walking, then paused and turned. Surely not?

'Emmy?' he asked. She nodded and smiled. 'Why Emmy! It's been such a long time!'

In that moment, Joshua's thoughts drifted back to their first encounter, on the ship that had brought them both from America to England.

Three Years Earlier

Joshua spotted a young girl leaning over the ship's rail, staring out across the vastness of the Atlantic. He assumed that, like himself, she was a slave or perhaps an indentured servant. This was the hour when those in steerage were permitted to exercise on deck.

'I guess that now we are so far from land, they must reckon we're not going to jump overboard,' said Joshua with a grin. The girl turned her head towards him, smiled and nodded. 'I know how to swim because, in Africa, I was a sailor, but that's beyond my capabilities,' Joshua continued. 'I'm going to be working on a farm in England. I don't reckon there will be much in the way of cotton growing there, thank the Lord! I tell you, I'm sure sick of pickin' cotton! Are you going to the countryside or the city?' The girl paused, stared back at him, then held up two fingers. Joshua was puzzled and thought for a moment. Then said, 'You mean the second one, the city?' The girl nodded. 'Say, you don't speak much, do you?' She shook her head and put her hand to her lips. 'Does that mean you can't speak?' She nodded once more. 'Well, I'll be damned! My name is Joshua. I can't think how I can guess yours.' She pointed to a piece of fabric pinned on her dress on which the word "Emmy" had been embroidered. 'Pleased to meet you, Emmy, and if you are wondering how come I can read, it's because my master loaned me to the Pastor for a year, and he taught me. Told me to keep it a secret because people don't want slaves getting too uppity, but he wanted me to read the Bible. Anyway, I can see it's going to take a little effort for us to be friends, but it's going to be worth it. We've got a long journey ahead.'

Over the course of the voyage, they indeed became friends. Between them, with Joshua being careful to phrase questions in such a way that Emmy could answer with a nod, or a shake of her head, or by flashing a big smile, and by Emmy using her hands to conjure words and ideas, they created their own private language and spent all the time they could together. Joshua worked out that Emmy was travelling to London to work as an indentured servant and had ten years left of her contract. Given that she would have to work for no wages, there would be very little difference between her working conditions and those of a slave.

'I bet people think that just because you can't speak, that you are stupid, but that isn't the case, is it?' laughed Joshua. Emmy smiled and nodded. She knew it was one factor that had led to her being employed indoors rather than out in the fields. It was almost as though she were invisible - she would take orders and quietly get on with her work. No one guarded what they said in front of her. Until she met Joshua, nobody had made the effort to communicate with her.

Because they had no duties on board, Joshua felt it was almost like being on holiday - not that he had ever had a vacation in his life. Admittedly, it was cold and wet on deck sometimes, but they managed to find shelter while they shared their stories.

'Did you ever speak?' asked Joshua. Emmy nodded. Then she made the action of rocking a baby. Tears came to her eyes, then she shook her head and looked away, unwilling to continue the conversation. Finally, that sad day arrived when the ship sailed up the River Mersey into Liverpool, signalling their time together was over. With one last wave, they walked away from the ship, following their respective owners. Joshua had never seen Emmy again until now.

There is only one item on the agenda, and that is to discuss what is happening in America and formulate our response,' declared Bellings, his tone cutting through the room with authority. 'General Truscott, you can start the proceedings.'

'Certainly, Sir. A little background first. As I am sure you know, the United States of America is divided into thirty-four states, but it intends to expand. Many more territories, such as Kansas and Nebraska, have not become states yet.'

'We know all that, Truscott! Do you think we are children? Get on with it!' interrupted Bellings impatiently, tapping his fingers on the polished wooden table.

'Erm...,' continued Truscott, nervously, 'Erm..however, in response to the recent election of Abraham Stamford as President on an anti-slavery ticket, first South Carolina and then six other southern states all seceded from the Union. They formed the Confederated States of America and elected Jefferson Melton President.'

'Yes, yes!' shouted Bellings, growing increasingly impatient. 'Bring us up to date!'

'Yes, Sir. Stamford declared war after the bombardment of a fort in South Carolina. And now, put simply, the South is fighting, amongst other things, to keep slavery, whereas the North wishes to abolish it.'

'And our official response is...?' Bellings demanded.

'It's neutral, Sir,' replied Major Truscott.

'And unofficially..?'

'If we put to one side any personal connections we may have with our friends in New York and Washington, the commodity we value is cotton imports from the South. Cities like Manchester depend on it. Let us discount any individual views we may have about the ethics of slavery; after all, it's been illegal here for some thirty years. Undoubtedly, our own industries, such as spinning, weaving and the manufacture of cotton goods, have become rich over recent years, so abolishing slavery would not be in the interests of the British people. Therefore, I would say, off the record, if we can, it is our patriotic duty to support the South.'

'Can they win?' asked Bellings.

'The North has more troops and money to finance the war, but the South has stronger motivation, and their army is better trained. Seven of the eight military colleges in America are in the South,' said Major Truscott, 'But unfortunately, the North has mounted a naval blockade, which is stopping the merchant ships from getting cotton to Great Britain.'

As the discussion continued, General Ridgley found himself doodling absentmindedly, lost in thought. If he wasn't a soldier, he would like to have been a war correspondent making sketches in the thick of the battle. He certainly had a talent for it. He drew lines of soldiers firing muskets at each other. One Union soldier reached to grab the flag from a dying comrade. The Confederate flag-bearer held his standard aloft. Ridgley had no idea what a Confederate flag might look like, so he based his design on the British flag and added a few stars. At the top of the page, he drew ships firing cannons at each other.

'What we need to do is orchestrate something that we can use as an excuse to bring us into the war on the side of the South,' mused Bellings.

'Orchestrate,' thought Ridgley, 'That's a good word,' and he duly wrote down the whole sentence.

'Perhaps one of our merchant ships could be attacked,' continued Bellings. Ridgley drew a sinking ship, with just its stern visible. Below it, he wrote, "HMS Great Britain ambushed by the Union".

'Ridgley!' boomed Bellings, plainly irritated. 'Must you keep scribbling?'

'Sorry, Sir.' Ridgley crumpled up the paper and tossed it at the waste paper basket on the other side of the room. It flew in without touching the sides. 'I say! What a shot!'

'Juvenile,' muttered Bellings angrily.

Thirty minutes later, the cabinet filed out of the office, nearly knocking over a maid, who had to jump smartly out of the way as they passed her.

'Fancy a brandy before the next meeting?' asked Truscott.

'Certainly do,' replied Ridgley, 'We can raise a toast to the prospect of war against the Americans!'

'How did you come to get this, Joshua?' asked Oliver, examining the doodles on the crumpled paper.

'Well, I've told you about my friend, Emmy. She's a cleaner in Westminster, and she found it in a waste paper basket after a government meeting. She wouldn't normally have paid any attention to it, but she overheard one of the Generals talking about Britain fighting against America as he left the room.'

'I thought you said she couldn't speak,' remarked Edward, raising an eyebrow.

'She can't, but I have ways of understanding her. Hand signs and acting things out and the like.' Edward examined the doodles and shook his head.

'These are hardly firm evidence of a government plot. On their own they wouldn't be enough to convince Reuters to publish a story. We need more.'

'I've asked Emmy to keep her ears open and bring me anything interesting. We usually eat at Mario's once a week. If she finds anything, I'll let you know,' promised Joshua.

'Isn't that just typical of Oliver!' complained Charlotte, her frustration evident in her voice. 'The night before we are due to fly to New York, he goes out drinking with his sailor friends. To make matters worse, he woke me up when he came in last night singing sea shanties.'

'He probably woke the whole hotel up,' laughed Sadie.

'I thought this was supposed to be a quiet hideaway! Fat chance of that!' continued Charlotte. 'Anyway, in fifteen minutes, we have to go, hangover or not. It's all arranged; young Tom has gone on ahead and taken a handcart loaded with supplies, and Craggs, the boatman, will be waiting to take us to the Rebel.'

'It's strange not having Genevieve with us. I've got used to her being around,' said Sadie.

'She will be quite happy in Paris,' said Jake. 'She gets very nervous during our little 'adventures'. She would rather be grappling with your sewing machine, Charlotte, than the controls of an airship.'

'Well, I love doing both,' said Charlotte with a determined nod. 'Billy, will you go and wake Sleeping Beauty?'

'You had better be ready to duck,' laughed Joshua, 'If you catch him in the middle of the wrong dream, he's likely to throw a punch!'

'Joshua, did you hear any more from your friend, Emmy?' asked Jake, 'Has she discovered any more secrets at the Houses of Parliament?'

'No, but I introduced her to Edward; he's going to meet her for tea twice a week, so if she discovers anything important, Edward can send a telegram to our hotel. He did tell me something, but I don't know if it will affect us. He says there's been fighting down in the South.'

'What about Texas?' asked Jake, 'That's in the South. Remember, we are going to America mainly because Texas has a supply of helium which could replace the hydrogen in the Rebel.'

'He says Texas isn't involved yet, but the situation may change. News is hard to come by. Finding out what's happening should be easier when we get to New York.'

At that moment, oblivious to Charlotte scowling at him, Oliver stumbled into the room. His eyes were red, he had a sheepish smile, and it appeared he had left the conscious part of his brain somewhere else, presumably in a dockside pub!

DAVE JOHNSON

CHAPTER THREE

Five Years ago: Savannah, Georgia

'Sit yourself down next to me, boy,' said Peter, gesturing to a chair. 'Work sure has been getting busy lately. I've been strugglin' to catch up with my own tail. Sooner we get you trained up, the better!'

'What do I have to do?' asked Paul, eager to learn.

'Just watch what I do for the moment. You can read 'n write can't you?

'Yes, Sir,'

'Where are you from, boy?'

'Right here in Savannah, Sir. My Pa's a boatbuilder, and my Grandpa has a small farm just out of town, but those ain't jobs for me. I'd rather earn my living with a pen.'

'If you've got brains, boy, you gotta use 'em. So, this

here's the ledger - the first column is for the date - it's the third of September, 1856. Next is a space for the name.'

'How do you know what they are called?'

'It don't matter what mumbo jumbo name they were called afore. I've got a list of names here, and I just use 'em up in order. This wench is Ruth. As long as I don't give the same name twice for the same buyer, then it don't matter. Hell, if you bought a cow and you wanted to call it Daisy, you wouldn't care if the farmer before called it Buttercup.'

'No, I suppose not. But, since bringing in slaves from Africa is against the law, surely these ones are already living in America. So haven't they already been given a Christian name?'

'Listen, boy, it doesn't do to be asking too many questions!'

'Do you write down a family name?'

'There you go again! Nope. There's no saying that a family is going to stay together. Look at it this way, farmer boy. If you was buying a couple of pigs to fatten up, you wouldn't be checking if they came from the same sow.'

'No Sir, but I'm not a farmer. That's my Grandpa.'

'Now, a word to the wise. Don't you go getting too close to 'em. It ain't no business of yours if the buyers want to give them a poke to see how strong they are, just as it ain't your concern if the sellers have covered 'em with grease to make 'em look more healthy. Look at it this way: if you was fattening up a goose, come Christmas, you would just kill it and eat it and throw away the bones on the trash heap. No use getting sentimental. There's a natural order of things; it's not like if your dog upped and died. You would bury the hound. What you see 'afore you are at the bottom of that natural order. Sentimentally, they don't rank any higher than that goose; the only difference is they are worth a lot more money.'

'I see, Sir. Actually, I don't live on a farm, you know.'

'So, now this sale is finished, here's where you write the new owner, Topper, and here is where you put down the price: three hundred and seventy dollars. I see this wench went for fifty dollars less than her brother, Luke, who Taggert bought. It's a good price, though. I'm sure they'll both fatten up nicely, and knowing Topper, I'm sure she'll fatten up in more ways than one!'

Two Years ago: Little Ridge, Georgia.

'Hey, Luke. I hear you're leavin',' said Old Matty.

'Leavin'? Nobody told me. Have I been sold?'

'No, I heard it from Martha, and she heard it from Jessy.'

'Jessy who works in the big house?'

'Yes, that's right. Missy Eveline is getting married, and you and Jessy are going with her as part of her dowry. You is goin' North.'

'Well, that's the first I've heard of it.'

'Luke!' yelled the overseer, sitting astride a chestnut horse, bullwhip in his hand. 'Get yer lazy black ass over here. Ya goin' to Calico Rise and if ya don't get a move on, I'll put another stripe on yer back!'

'I guess you just been told,' chuckled Old Matty.

'It sure is a long way to Calico Rise,' complained Jessy from the back of the covered wagon.

'It ain't so bad for you. At least your legs aren't tied up.'

'That's 'cause I ain't gonna go running off like some damn fool crazy negro like you.'

'I ain't gonna go runnin' off. There's nothing out there except prairie. Where am I gonna go? Anyways, the wagon driver and his partner have got rifles; they'd shoot me. That's if the injuns don't get me first.'

'I heard the wagon driver tell Missy Eveline that there ain't no injuns round these parts.'

'Sure is hot and stuffy back here. No wonder Missy Eveline is sitting up front.' Suddenly, a gunshot rang out, followed by a scream, and Eveline tumbled into the back of the wagon.

'Outlaws,' she gasped, 'Cody's been killed.'

'I'll try and outrun them,' yelled Danny from his seat at the front of the wagon as he whipped the horses into a gallop. 'Can you shoot a rifle, Ma'am? Cody's rifle is by his side. I can't drive and shoot straight.'

'Give me a gun,' cried Luke.

'Ain't givin' no guns to no negroes,' Danny shouted back. They were the last words he ever spoke as a bullet entered his brain, and he slumped over. Meanwhile, the horses continued to race across the prairie.

'Gun, quick!' yelled Luke. Eveline had no misgivings about arming slaves. She scrambled to the front of the wagon and threw back two rifles. 'And pass me a knife, Miss Eveline.'

'Do you know how to fire it?' screamed Jessy.

'I only seen it done,' replied Luke. 'Pull the trigger to shoot, and then pull down the guard. It's like a lever that loads another bullet.'

Eveline had seen their pursuers gaining on them and was shaking with fear. Her eyes were screwed shut. Luke set to work sawing through the rope that bound his wrist to the wagon's side. At first, the wagon was in danger of overturning as it bounced and careered along the track, but gradually, the horses began to slow down. Then Jessy gasped as the silhouette of a man was framed in the wagon's entrance. The outlaw paused for a moment, and then he saw Jessy, holding the rifle in trembling hands. He raised his and cocked back the trigger. Luke may never have fired a gun, but he knew how to use a knife, and without hesitation, he threw the knife at their adversary, and it buried itself in the man's chest. Silently, the outlaw toppled over, trapping Eveline beneath him. It was just as well that Jessy hadn't fired the gun because it would have alerted the man they could now hear climbing onto the wagon. He peered inside and saw his friend lying on top of a struggling young girl.

'Hey! You better save some for me,' he laughed. Then Jessy pulled the trigger, and a deafening roar echoed within the wagon. Eveline screamed, adding to the confusion. Now, two dead men lay sprawled inside. Luke yanked at his wrist, breaking the last few strands that secured it, and shuffled forward, his feet still tied together. Luke grabbed the other rifle and pointed it at the opening. The only sound came from the wagon itself, as it creaked and rumbled at a walking pace. Jessy crawled to the front of the wagon to peer fearfully outside.

'I can't see no one else,' she said with a tremor.

Luke rolled the man he had killed over and retrieved the knife. Ignoring the blood all over it, he began sawing furiously through the rope knotted around his legs. Eveline was wide-eyed in stunned silence now, blood staining the front of her dress. Eventually, Luke was free, and gun in hand, he crept out into the daylight, keeping as low as possible. He scanned the horizon in all directions, then gave a nervous laugh and stood up. They were alone, save for two riderless horses grazing nearby.

'There was only two of 'em,' he shouted. 'Come on out.'

Ten minutes later, they stood looking at the four bodies laid in a line on the grass.

'Now what do we do?' asked Jessy. 'I suppose you and your black ass are heading for the hills,' she said, glaring at Luke.

'I told you, I ain't gonna do that. Anyway, there aren't any hills - we're on the prairie. I don't reckon we've got time to bury them. Them two outlaws might be members of a gang. Who knows if some more of 'em aren't right behind 'em.'

'It's quicker to carry on than to turn back. Jed said we only had another day to travel,' commented Eveline.

'Is this the same Jed that said we were safe to travel around these parts?' asked Luke.

'Shhh!' Jessy rolled her eyes to the sky, 'Remember, you is still a slave!' she hissed. Eveline smiled.

'Thank you for saving my life,' she said.

'We aint safe yet,' replied Jessy, 'I hope you know how to ride a wagon 'cause I sure don't, and this lazy black-assed fool don't know half as much as he thinks!'

'I've never steered anything as big as this before, but I think I can control the horses,' replied Eveline, 'I'm not travelling with dead bodies inside, but it doesn't seem right to leave them here.'

Luke solved the problem by capturing the outlaws'

horses and tethering them to the back of the wagon. Then, amid a tirade of cussing and much huffing and puffing, he hauled the four dead men up to lie face down across the horses' backs. Then the wagon and its gruesome escort continued on its way.

After spending another night on the prairie, during which Luke was the only one who slept well, the wagon finally rolled into Calico Rise late in the evening of the next day. A cowboy rode alongside them, spat on the ground, and then gave them a lopsided smile with a mouth full of blackened teeth.

'Well lookee here, Two negras and a purty young gal. I'll guide you to the hoor house if you want, and I'll see you later.' Eveline held the reins, while the two slaves sat on either side of her. Luke patted the rifle on his lap, making sure the cowboy knew he was armed.

'I am looking for the residence of Major Bannock,' said Eveline in a steely voice.

'She's going to be his bride,' said Jessy proudly.

'Oh sorry, Ma'am,' stuttered the cowboy, realising he had overstepped the mark, 'The Bannock place is a mile on down the road on the left. You can't miss it. It's a big white house with pillars and everythin' fancy,' and he slowed his horse down, dropping back in the hope that they wouldn't remember him. After all, the Bannocks were an important family around these parts. It was then that he noticed the horses hitched to the back of the wagon and their lifeless riders. 'Oh! You better call in at the Sheriff's office in the middle of town first, though. Looks like you got some explainin' to do.' The cowboy pulled on his reins and paused, watching the procession trundle into town.

'Thank you for the friendly welcome to town,' shouted back Luke, 'I'm looking forward to spending some time with you. You know, playing some cards, spinning a few yarns, three fingers of whisky, maybe you could take me to the...'

'Shhh!' hissed Jessy, 'Remember, you is still a slave!'

Eighteen Months Ago
'We're going to move further North.' said Jessy to Luke. 'I can see why Mrs B would want me to come, but I can't think for the life of me why the Major should want to haul your lazy black ass all the way to Washington, even though you ain't a slave no more.'

'I'll have you know that the Major is trainin' me to be a valet an' he says I'm getting to be very good at it!'

'Well, you sure weren't much good at picking cotton, or doing most anythin' else, come to think of it. This time, we'll have soldiers guarding us, so don't expect to be killing any more outlaws. We got ourselves our freedom that day by rescuing Mrs B, but believe me, you've gone as far as you're gonna go!'

'Washington! Ain't that where the President lives? That's as high as I wanna go.'

'A black man as President?' laughed Jessy, 'Wait a moment, did I just see a pig fly past?'

One Year Ago
'So how's a Southern farm boy like you gettin' on in this here capital?' asked Jessy, 'I don't see so much of you

these days.'

'I tell you, my life's a heap more comfortable than it was back in the old times,' replied Luke. 'However, I don't know how much you know about the outside world now you are livin' in the big house, but life's not a bed o' roses for us coloured folk in general. I had some time on my hands, so I explored the city, and I found myself in Willow Tree Alley. That is one tough, wicked district. There's little work, even less money, and a whole mess of families are squeezed into some pretty awful houses, some no better than dog kennels. How's it for you with Mrs B?'

'I'm happy for the ways things have turned out. I spend my time in grand surroundings, but I's worried things is goin' to change on account of they say war is coming.'

'Is that true?' asked Luke, 'I've been hearin' rumours, and I was wondrin' why the Major was spending so much time in meetings. Who we gonna fight and why?'

'I gets to overhear some of the army wives talkin',' replied Jessy, 'What they's sayin' is that the Southern States have left the Union, and the Northern States is goin' to go down and force them to come back. It's all 'cause of people like you and me.'

'It ain't my fault. I get the blame for everythin' around here!'

No. I mean 'cause of slaves. The South is fearin' that the Union is going to abolish slavery.'

'Well, I'll be damned! They's gonna fight a war over little old me. Wait a moment. They've made a mistake. I'm a free man!'

'You is now. But if there's a war and the South wins, then your days of freedom might be over, and your lazy black ass will be back pickin' cotton!'

Six Months ago

'You is what?' In a flash, Jessy was the angriest that Luke had ever seen her.

'I said I'm gonna enlist. They're forming a regiment just for coloured soldiers.'

'I ain't met anyone as stupid as you,' fumed Jessy, 'Why do you think they is doing that? It's because this war ain't goin' the way they thought it would. Them Yankee Generals thought it would be a walkover, but it ain't so. Now they's thinking, let the coloured boys stop the bullets first, and when they ain't doing that, they can do all the dirty work that no one else will do. The idea of you going to fight is the dumbest thing I ever heard. You escaped from the South, and now you're plannin' on going back! What do you think they will do to you if they catch you? They'll string you up with a sign round your neck saying, 'Here hangs one stupid black-assed fool.'

'I knows all that, Jessy. I ain't never told you, but I got a sister, Amara. We was sold to different farms. I don't know where she is. My English wasn't too good at the time so I couldn't follow what was happening. I don't even know what her English name is. I was sold first so they dragged me away. Anyway, I reckon she will still be a slave and I ain't sayin' I can go and free her, but maybe I can help free others like her and then I won't feel guilty 'bout this easy life I've been having.'

Last month
"Dear Jessy

This is the first letter that I ever wrote and I must admit that I got a little help with the spelling from a friend, but the words are all mine. I'm not going to talk much about the war because it don't make for pretty readin'. I want to thank you for the letter that you wrote me and to tell you how much it means to know that there is someone who cares for me. I have been in quite a few battles now. Yes, never mind what people was saying - they have given guns to us coloured troops! But the point is, I have seen a lot of men die, and I don't know how come I am still alive, but it's got me thinking that if I don't tell you now that I love you and always have, then I may never get the chance to say it.

From your black-assed lovin' fool."

CHAPTER FOUR

New York: the corner of 6th Avenue and 11th Street.

'It's not hard to see why they call it the Grapevine,' said Charlotte, looking up at the thick, luxurious vine growing up one side of a three-storey clapboard building. 'You go in first, Joshua. Oliver and Billy should already be here. Oliver wanted to sample the ale, and Billy's been looking forward to tasting the famous mutton pies.'

Joshua pushed open the swinging saloon doors and paused momentarily, his eyes trying to adjust to the dim lighting as he scanned the bar, searching for Oliver and Billy amongst the crowd. One voice cut through the general hubbub of the saloon.

'Jamie, since when have you started serving blacks?'

Joshua stared the man who had spoken fully in the eye. He noticed a twitch in the man's left cheek, which became more pronounced the longer they maintained eye contact. Unaccountably, Joshua was consumed by a feeling of dread. The bartender didn't answer the question but addressed Sadie and Charlotte.

'We don't serve women here. This is a respectable establishment!'

'Charming! We don't want to stay where we're not welcome anyway!' announced Sadie, and she grabbed hold of Joshua's arm, wheeled him round, and to the sound of laughter, they left the Grapevine.

They stood for a moment outside before Billy came bursting through the door.

'They bleedin' well laughed at Jake for ordering milk,' he said. 'It's certainly a lively place. Lots of chat. It's funny, but we've been talkin' to that geezer wot shouted out, an' he seemed alright.'

'Do you know his name?' asked Joshua.

'They call him Double Top,' answered Billy. 'He's full of stories, mostly tellin' how he's born lucky an' always comes out a bleedin' winner.' Joshua solemnly nodded as he took in this information.

'Have you had your pie, Billy?' asked Sadie.

'No, we was waiting until you got here.'

'You go in and have it. We'll find something else to eat here in Greenwich Village and come back in an hour,' she replied.

Later, as they walked along, looking for somewhere to sit and eat the bread and ham they had bought, Sadie commented:

'You're quiet, Joshua. 'It's unusual for you to be upset by a bit of name-calling. "Water off a duck's back" is what you usually say.'

'I know that man,' he replied, 'It was a long time ago, but I'll never forget him. Sit down here on the grass, and I will tell you about him. My first owner in South Carolina hit upon some hard times. His family died of consumption, and cutworms attacked the cotton crop, so he decided to sell up and return to Scotland. He realised he wouldn't get a good price if he sold his slaves locally, as everyone knew his circumstances. The local farmers would fix the prices because they knew it was a forced sale and then probably resell at a profit.

So the nine of us were handed over to an agent, and we were marched secretly to Georgia to be sold at an auction in Savannah. We had to cross the Blue Ridge Mountains, and the paths were cold, wet, and slippery. I was pretty fit, but even I found it a long and tiring walk. The agent didn't care. He and his two hands were riding horses, and they had thick coats on whilst we just had the threadbare, cotton clothes that we wore out in the fields. Some of us didn't even have shoes.

Anyway, one day, I pleaded with the agent to let us rest up for a while. 'Please, Master Top,' I said. I'd heard the two hands calling him Double Top, but it turned out that he didn't like me using it. He stared at me for a while. I reckon he was wondering what to do with me, and I saw that twitch of his getting stronger the more angry he became. The hands aimed their guns at me as Double Top climbed off his horse. I realise now that he didn't want to disfigure me in some way because that might affect the price he got for me. He would have been in line for a cut of the profits. At the time, I thought he was going to kill me, but instead, he punched me hard in the stomach several times until I could hardly breathe. Then he drew his gun and watched whilst the two other men repeated the punishment.

There were some other incidents. We had to sleep around a campfire at night. The hands took turns to guard us, but Double Top had a tent, and on several occasions, he made one of the women join him for the night. They weren't willing, but they had no choice.

We eventually stumbled into Savannah, were made to wash the trail dust off in the river, and locked in a barn until the auction. The last time I saw him, he was counting his money after the sale. So that's the tale of me and Double Top. He won't remember me. I was just one of hundreds of slaves he had dealings with, but I certainly remember him!'

When they arrived back at the Grapevine, Sadie was still angry after hearing Joshua's story. Charlotte was glad that Sadie had left her Glove back in the hotel because if she hadn't, she would undoubtedly have marched straight into the bar and shot a dart through Double Top's heart and then who knows what trouble they would all have been in.

Oliver, Jake and Billy eventually tumbled out of the bar.

'That was an interesting experience,' slurred Oliver, 'I think I'll have to return.'

'Isn't beer the same from one pub to the next?' asked Charlotte.

'First of all, you couldn't be further from the truth, but that's not why I want to go back. You couldn't imagine the range of different conversations I've had.'

'It's true,' said Jake, 'Oliver seemed to get on with

everyone. Sometimes, he was laughing and joking with people, and sometimes, he was in a corner whispering.'

'If you want to know what's going on in New York, then that's the place to find out,' said Oliver.

'So, what have you learned?' asked Charlotte.

'This little dispute down in the South, the Union Army against the Confederates, is not going so well. It won't be over any time soon. Thousands of soldiers have been killed on both sides. It's not as straightforward as North versus South, though, as there are many Confederate sympathisers here in New York. I reckon that bar is full of Confederate spies.'

'And what of Double Top? Surely he's not become a Unionist?' demanded Sadie.

He claims he's a neutral businessman,' said Oliver, 'But I'm certain there's more to him than meets the eye.'

'He was bloomin' pally wiv you,' observed Billy, 'I don't fink 'e connected you wiv Joshua.'

'True, and for the moment, let's keep him ignorant of our united band of brothers and sisters. I'm curious about him, and I think we'll get more out of him if he remains in the dark. He's interested in me because he sees me as neutral.'

'Nuffink to do wiv the fact that you kept buying him drinks then?' laughed Billy.

'It's true; I was perhaps a little profligate with my purse, but I wanted to whet his appetite. He wants to meet me to talk about selling me bonds.'

'What's a bleedin' bond when it's at home?' asked Billy.

'It's when you buy a document from a company, or even from a country, and get paid interest each year. Then, after an agreed amount of time, you get your money back.'

'Cor blimey. Money for old rope!'

'There are risks. Companies that pay you the kind of interest Double Top was talking about are more likely to go bust. Also, you have to ask yourself, what are they doing with that influx of cash? They aren't giving you interest payments out of the goodness of their hearts. Someone has to benefit, and I suspect that person is Double Top!' said Oliver.

'Jake, you've been rather quiet,' commented Sadie. 'I can't see you getting interested in the world of high finance!'

'As you might have gathered, there are all sorts of different people in there, and I was having an interesting discussion with an engineer about the best welding techniques to create a water-tight seal for a project he was about to start. He knew Double Top as well,' replied Jake.

'Me? I didn't get much talkin' done 'cause my norf an' South was full of mutton pie. I 'ad four of 'em an' bleedin' delicious they were too,' said Billy. 'But I tell you one fing. I wouldn't trust that Double Top as far as I could frow 'im!'

It was early morning, and Joshua rubbed his hands together to warm them, regretting leaving his monogrammed leather gloves in his hotel room. He leant over the parapet from which he had a good view of the East River and New York's dockland. Before his time as a slave, Joshua had been a fisherman in Africa, so he was always drawn to scenes of maritime activity. Joshua could see the dockworkers lined up, hoping to get chosen by the foreman for a day's work, and decided to take a closer look. He knew he wouldn't be mistaken for a stevedore or a longshoreman as he was too well-dressed for that kind of employment, although there was a time when he would have jumped at the offer of such work.

A burly foreman inspected the line, pointing at those he wanted. Joshua noticed several black faces amongst the hopeful workers, but he also noticed that the foreman invariably chose the white workers. Eventually, the foreman filled his quota and turned, leading his selected men towards the ships moored on the docks. Gradually, the disappointed hopefuls on the quayside dispersed, muttering amongst themselves.

'It's been two weeks since I picked up any work!'

'He always chooses the Irish. We Italians hardly ever get chosen.'

'At least we get picked before the negroes.'

Joshua smiled at a dejected young man.

'Hard luck,' Joshua said. He wasn't surprised that the foreman hadn't chosen this young man because he was not only black but also slightly built. Joshua towered over him. All those selected had been big, strong-looking workers.

'I'm surprised you didn't get picked,' said the young man.

'I wasn't looking for work; I'm just a spectator. I couldn't sleep, so I got up early. My name's Joshua.'

'And I'm Isaac.'

'Good to meet you, Isaac, where do you live?'

'Unfortunately, I live on the Five Points.'

'Why "unfortunately"? I don't know where that is.'

'If you saw it, you would know what I mean. It's one of the worst areas of New York; It's in Lower Manhattan.' Just then, a voice Joshua recognised rang out:

'Hey, you. Are you looking for work?' Joshua turned around, and his eyes met those of Double Top. He felt as though his blood had curdled. Joshua's nemesis showed no signs of recognising him from the day before.

'Not you. You're too big and bulky,' Double Top said, dismissing him, 'It's this young fella I'm interested in.' Joshua retreated, sat on a wall and watched the two converse. Eventually, they parted company and Joshua called Isaac over to him.

'Hey,' said Isaac with a broad smile on his face. 'I've been offered a day's work. Good money, too. I don't know what I have to do. He will tell me on the day, but he said I have to keep it a secret.'

'Well, I already know about it, so you can tell me,' said Joshua.

'He only really asked me two questions. He wanted to know if I had strong arms, which I have, and then he asked me if I was frightened of being in small spaces, which I'm not. Ha! If you saw my room, you would know that!'

'It's all very interesting. I wonder why the secrecy,' said Joshua, 'Do you mind letting me know as soon as you get more information?' Isaac nodded. 'Good! Come, let me buy you breakfast. I saw a place nearby with macaroni and ham chalked on a blackboard. Maybe they'll make us egg fritters, too. Ha ha, perhaps you'd better not eat too much, or you'll be no good for this job that's only suitable for skinny young fellas.'

CHAPTER FIVE

As Isaac strolled along the dockside, the sight of the warehouse before him struck a stark contrast to the others he had passed. Weathered and forsaken, its dilapidated clapboard and shattered windows exuded an air of neglect that offered little reassurance for Isaac's prospects of employment. Double Top and a small group of men were congregated just outside the entrance.

'Good, you're all here now. I hope you've told no one about this meeting because if you have, the work might all fall through,' said Double Top.

Everyone shook their heads, although Isaac felt a little guilty because he had told Joshua and knew he was waiting nearby. 'You may have noticed that you are all men of colour,' continued Double Top, 'That's because I have long been a supporter of your race.'

'That contradicts the tales Joshua told me about you,' thought Isaac.

'Follow me. We'll get you trained up.' Double Top led the way up a rickety staircase to a room at the back of the warehouse, where Isaac was surprised to find the group had to carry out their morning's work seated on a row of chairs in front of which was mounted a long cranked structure.

'It's simple,' explained Double Top. 'What we have here is a model of the actual machine you'll be operating. It won't be in a room like this; you will be enclosed, which is why I asked you if you were frightened of small spaces. I want to see if you have the strength to turn that crankshaft in unison for one hour.'

Later, Joshua treated Isaac to lunch at Downing's Oyster House.

'I can't fathom it,' said Isaac. 'He's given us a dollar, though, and we have to report to the docks every day next week. What's more, if we turn up and we aren't needed that day, he'll give us twenty-five cents for doing nothing!'

'I'm going to discuss this with Jake; he's the one with the brains, so let's see if he can puzzle it out,' replied Joshua.

'I've been giving this a lot of thought,' said Jake to the other Rebel Runaways gathered in Oliver's hotel room. It was a little cramped, but they hadn't wanted to meet in a restaurant or bar for fear of being overheard. 'First of all, there's Double Top. We know he's likely to be a Confederate sympathiser, possibly even a spy, so all the secrecy surrounding this operation probably has nothing to do with restricting the numbers to a hand-picked few, as Double Top led Isaac to believe, but is actually a scheme aimed at harming the Union cause.'

'That's a fair assumption,' said Oliver.

'Then I thought to myself,' continued Jake, 'What is the purpose of the crankshaft?'

'Could it be powering some kind of factory machinery?' asked Sadie.

'A good suggestion,' replied Jake, 'But why use men when you've got steam? And ask yourselves this: why meet at the docks?'

'To get on a bleedin' ship, or maybe to wait for one to come in,' suggested Billy.

'Exactly! I think they are waiting for one, which is why they don't know when the work will start. You usually know when a ship will set off, but you don't know exactly when it will arrive. It depends on the weather conditions. Then, I don't know why, but I thought back to a conversation I had in the Grapevine with an engineer who was investigating water-tight welding seals. The engineer was a little drunk, so maybe he wasn't supposed to talk about the project, but the combination of beer and a chance meeting with someone like me who was genuinely interested loosened his tongue. Then I pictured him in a quiet corner, whispering his secrets to Double Top. By putting all these elements together with the fact that the men will be in a confined space, I came up with something incredible. I think Isaac will be going to sea inside a metal craft submerged below the waves, and the crankshaft will turn the propeller. The Confederates have invented a submersible boat!'

'But why?' asked Sadie.

'That I don't know. We will have to keep our ears to the ground.' Jake said. 'And I'm going to figure out how to stop it.'

'Cor blimey, how can you stop a boat that's under the bleedin' water?' asked Billy.

'Same way you catch a fish,' replied Jake with a smile.

'Wiv a fishin' rod?'

'No. With a net.'

'I wonder if there are any clues in the newspaper about what they are up to,' mused Oliver and he started to leaf through the New York Herald. 'My God!' he gasped.

'What is it?' asked Charlotte with concern. Oliver looked aghast.

'I've just seen something in the paper, and it's jogged my memory. Do you remember that I met our old friend Nathan before we left England…'

'How could we forget?' interrupted Charlotte dryly. You didn't sober up for two days.'

'…and how on the next day I knew there was something that Nathan told me, but I couldn't remember what it was?' continued Oliver, ignoring Charlotte's disapproving tone, 'Well, I haven't given it a moment's thought until now. Until I saw that!' Oliver pointed at the newspaper.

'It's a warning about not discussing secrets because of Confederate spies,' said Jake, studying the paper.

'Better clamp yer mouth shut when yer goes down the Grapevine then,' laughed Billy.

'It's, not what it says; it's the illustration.'

'It's a flag. Whose flag is that? I've not seen it before.' said Charlotte.

'I gather it's the flag of the newly confederated states, so you're not going to see it flying from any flagpoles in New York,' replied Oliver, 'I told you Nathan was going to be sailing a cargo ship, the Albion, to New York. In fact, he will be at sea now. Nathan described a flag that he had been given, a red and white one, and it was just like this one in the newspaper. The shipping agent told Nathan that it was a trading pennant, signifying cooperation between America and Britain, so he should take down the Union Jack and fly the new one when he was close to New York. Moreover, Nathan was mystified because he was to sail all the way to New York with an empty hold. That's never done!'

Jake's mind was whirring.

'Do you think the aim is for the Albion to provoke a response from the Union Navy and that the submersible could be involved?'

'I think you've hit the nail on the head,' said Oliver grimly.

'But why?' asked Sadie, confused.

'Many in Great Britain would like to side with the Southern States to protect their interests in the cotton industry. If an international incident occurred, it might give them an excuse to abandon neutrality,' replied Oliver. Just then, there was a knock on the door. Joshua reached it first.

'Telegram,' sang out a young boy, who hovered, waiting for a tip. Oliver obliged, read the telegram, and then announced:

'It's from Edward. He says Joshua's friend, Emmy, found another doodle in a waste basket. It was a drawing of a ship in distress and was captioned "Albion Destined for a Watery Grave".'

'Then that bleedin' well proves it,' exclaimed Billy, 'Jake, you're a bloomin' genius!'

'But surely if Union sailors boarded Nathan's ship, he would tell them he wasn't a Confederate?' protested Sadie.

'That's if he were alive to tell the tale,' answered Oliver. 'Anyway, I'm off to the Grapevine.'

'But it's only nine o'clock in the morning,' protested

Charlotte.

'It's the best place I can think of to find Double Top. There's no time like the present!'

'But...' Charlotte's voice trailed off, she suspected Oliver simply wanted a drink.

'Sometimes, you have to grasp the nettle!' asserted Oliver.

'So, is your brain so addled you can only speak in idioms now?' asked Charlotte.

'Ha ha, Many a true word is spoken in jest!' quipped Oliver, heading for the door.

'Hold on! I'm coming with you!'

'Jake!' said Charlotte, pretending to be shocked, 'He's leading you up the garden path!'

'Cor blimey, I got it!' exclaimed Billy once Oliver and Jake had left, 'You're all talkin' in bloomin' proverbs!'

'Better late than never!' laughed Sadie.

Unlike Oliver, Jake didn't plan on staying long in the Grapevine. He was pleased to find the engineer, Sam, eating breakfast inside. Jake ordered scrambled eggs and joined him. They talked earnestly about their love of scientific exploration, and Jake was able to quiz Sam casually about his current project without rousing suspicion. Later, as he left the bar, armed with the information he needed, Jake thought ruefully to himself:

'It's a terrible thing, war. Apart from all the death and destruction, it puts folk who otherwise might have been great friends on opposite sides of the conflict. Sam and I have a lot in common. He is genuinely interested in my metal hand from an engineering point of view, and I am intrigued by the submersible that I believe he's designed.

But, perhaps through allegiance to the state where he was born, he's helping a cause that supports slavery. What's ironic is that he's given me the name and address of the best supplier of clockwork parts, and I intend to use them to build something to defeat his invention!'

Oliver had to wait longer to meet his quarry, but spending hours in a bar was hardly an ordeal for him. It was well after five o'clock when Double Top breezed in.

'Topsy, me old friend,' slurred Oliver. Double Top looked across at Oliver and smiled. He was happy to see Oliver not only because was he was good company, but also it was easier to do business with men who were intoxicated. He didn't realise that Oliver was quite used to functioning in that condition, although remembering his actions the following day might prove difficult. Oliver wasn't sure what his aim was in befriending Double Top. In an echo of Jake's relationship with Sam, Double Top was ordinarily just the type of man Oliver liked to spend time with in a bar. He thought it might be useful to know where Double Top was staying. It took very little effort to find out because Double Top invited Oliver to accompany him there.

'We'll have one more drink, Oliver, and then come with me to my hotel. I've something to show you. You know those bonds I was talking about? They're a sure-fire means of getting rich quickly, and I have some that I can put your way. Keep it secret, mind, or else everyone will want them.'

'Keeping secrets is hardly difficult when you don't remember anything, is it!' scolded Charlotte, looking down at Oliver, who was lying fully clothed on his bed. 'You haven't even taken your boots off. How much did you drink?' Oliver groaned and rubbed his forehead.

'Ah! I'm afraid I can't remember that either.'

'Whilst you have been out boozing, Jake has been working all day and night on his new invention.'

'Wait a moment; when my head clears a little, I should be able to tell you the good news.'

'Good news?'

'Yes, I remember I was feeling pretty pleased with myself. Ah! I know. I found out where Double Top is staying.'

'Good! Where is it?'

'Oh, that I can't remember,' replied Oliver, but as Charlotte's face fell, he continued, 'But I picked up a card from the counter in reception. I put it in my wallet. Here it is.'

'Well, that's something, but what's that?' asked Charlotte, indicating a document that Oliver was unfolding. 'And I can't seem to see any money in your purse. Did you spend it all on drink?'

'No, but there was quite a lot of money in there when I went out,' said Oliver, studying the certificate in his hands, 'I seem to have bought myself a bond. It's funded by a bank in a city called Savannah!'

CHAPTER SIX

'It's today!' Joshua was breathless from racing back from the docks, 'I stayed long enough to see a merchant seaman rowing Isaac and his companions out to a boat in the harbour, then I rushed back to tell you all.'

'At last! Rebels, we are ready to go! If it had happened a few days ago, it would have been a different matter, but we are all set; I've finished making the new equipment,' replied Jake, with a mixture of pride and relief.

Thirty minutes later, the crew were assembled outside Trinity Church, the tallest building in New York, watching Joshua climb out of a window clutching a rope that he had stowed there in advance. He swung away from the steeple, then shimmied up to the Rebel's gondola, from where he released a rope ladder, enabling the rest of the Rebel

Runaways to climb up to the airship.

As usual, Charlotte was the pilot as they followed the course of the East River heading for the sea.

Out of sight from the Rebel, The Albion was approaching America.

'Shall I run this fancy flag up the mast now, Captain,' asked the First Mate.

'Yes, I can see an American warship on the horizon,' replied Nathan, 'I've been at sea a long time, but I ain't never seen a flag like this'un before. Still, better show them we are friendly.'

'And what about the Union Jack?'

'The shipping agent said we should take it down. I don't like it, but that's what he said. There are lots of things about this trip giving me an uneasy feeling, deep down in my bones. For instance, sailing here with an empty hold and having no documentation about what cargo we are picking up. The shipping agent seemed a bit shifty, too. I ain't never seen him before. At least with nothing to unload, we'll get onto dry land quicker and we can wet our whistles in a New York tavern. Come boys, let's sing.'

'Now rouse her right up boys for New York town,' sang the First Mate.

'Go way, way, blow the man down,' came the refrain from the crew.

'We'll blow the man up and blow the man down,' sang the First Mate.

'Oh, give us some time to blow the man down.'

In the crow's nest of the American ship, the Guardian, a sailor lowered his telescope and shouted down to an officer on the deck:

'Ship approaching, Sir. It's too far away for me to identify their flag.'

'We'll investigate; we can't get too complacent with all these rumours about Confederate spies flying around,' the officer thought to himself. He returned to the bridge and instructed the helmsman, 'A ship's coming our way; turn into the wind. Let's slow down and wait for them.'

'Who's that?' asked the helmsman, gesturing to another ship following behind them.

'That's the Osprey. We inspected her yesterday. She's carrying some strange-looking machinery bound for England. Ignore her.'

Aboard the Osprey, Isaac was terrified. Being on the ship evoked memories of the tales his grandfather had told about the long, horrific journey when the slavers had brought him to America from Africa. He looked at a long metal cylinder suspended from a gantry above the deck with suspicion and disbelief.

'Do you mean we have to climb inside that? Surely there's not enough room for all of us.'

'Yes, you do, and yes, there is,' barked Double Top. 'Let me remind you that the Osprey is conducting an important scientific mission on behalf of the Government, and anyone who jeopardises it will be dealt with most severely!' To emphasise the point, he drew back his jacket and patted a pistol secured in a leather holster.

Charlotte was flying the airship at full speed.

'Billy, Sadie, Joshua, help me with the net, please,' called Jake. 'I don't want it to get twisted up. When the time comes, we must throw it out of the door, each holding onto one of my clockwork tadpoles.'

'They do look like giant tadpoles,' laughed Sadie, 'Do they really swim?'

'They do,' replied Jake proudly, 'I tested them in the bath. They will each swim away from the centre of the net.

Actually, it's more like a giant hammock, and as you can see, it's made of rigging, not fishing net, as we have a particularly fat and heavy fish to catch. So my tadpoles will not only keep the hammock taut, but they will also make it sink so we can scoop up the submersible. Billy and I wound them up fully, so we just have to press a button on top to start them before we throw them out of the gondola.'

'Oliver, are you sure the Rebel will be powerful enough to lift the submersible?' asked Charlotte, worriedly.

'I'm fairly confident it will,' replied Oliver.

'Only fairly?

'Well, it probably will. Possibly will... perhaps.'

'Cor blimey. Yer makin' it sound bleedin' worse. I fink you should keep yer bloomin' trap shut, if it's all the same, Oliver. Yer givin' me the willies!'

Double Top was completing the final preparations for the Osprey's mission. He had shepherded Isaac and his companions into the submersible and it was now dangling from a crane a few feet above the deck.

'Nobody told us it would be dark,' protested Isaac. 'They should have had us practising with our eyes closed!'

'You ain't helping. Just do as you're told,' said Ethan, who had been appointed as commander. It was his job to steer, and ensure that the six-foot docking rod made contact with the Guardian's wooden hull.

'I don't know how it attaches itself to the ship, but Double Top said it will, and he must know what he's talking about.'

On deck, Double Top continued to give orders:

'Now they are all inside, you can bring out the torpedo and fasten it to the end of...what did I call it? I know, the docking rod. Careful, boys; it's highly explosive. It will go off if it makes contact with anything, and that includes you,

you clumsy oaf! As soon as the torpedo is secure, you can lower the submersible into the sea on the blind side. The crew have been told to count to ten before they start turning the crankshaft to give us a chance to get out of the way.'

Meanwhile, aboard the Albion:

'Looks like we've got a welcome party,' called Nathan. 'Sing out, boys, sing out!'

'I fear not the weather, I fear not the sea
I remember the fallen... do they think of me?
When their bones in the ocean, forever will be'

If anyone on the Osprey, the Guardian or the Albion had looked to the sky, back towards New York, they may have noticed an airship approaching.

'Now this looks interesting,' remarked Oliver, training his telescope on the distant sails. 'I suspect the ship sailing West is Nathan's; the biggest one looks like a Union warship, and that third ship loitering near the warship is probably the one carrying the submersible. Fly as fast as you can, Charlotte.'

'It strikes me that, while we might know what is happening, neither the warship nor the Albion will have a clue,' said Charlotte. 'I wonder if we would have time to lower someone down and put them in the picture before they start taking pot-shots at us.'

'I could go down to the Albion and get them to lower that Confederate flag. I can see it now,' said Oliver, lowering his telescope. 'You fly the Rebel better than I do, Charlotte. Besides, I'd like to get down there in the thick of the action.'

'If you could leave the helm for a moment, Charlotte, to help throw out the tadpoles, then we can spare someone else to go down to the Osprey,' said Jake.

'I can set the controls to fly automatically,' replied Charlotte.

'Then I'll go,' said Joshua.

'No, you ruddy well won't! I'll go,' said Sadie indignantly.

'It might be dangerous!' protested Joshua.

'Don't you be so bloody patronisin'!' retorted Sadie.

'Now, now! She has a point; I've seen her fire those darts of hers,' laughed Oliver, 'She's lethal!'

'And they won't be threatened by me as a mere woman,' Sadie said sarcastically, glancing at Joshua.

'Come on now; we are a team, and it's almost time to go. Any sign of the submersible, Charlotte?'

'Oh no! I think they have already launched it; I can see a dark shape, like a large fish, heading towards the warship. We've got time, though. Just! Get ready, Sadie.'

Billy threw the rope ladder out of the door, and without a moment's hesitation, Sadie flung the bag containing her dart-firing glove around her neck and climbed out of the gondola.

'Sir, look up there, Sir,' cried the First Mate of the Guardian. Her crew had been so intent on tracking the progress of the advancing ship that they hadn't noticed the arrival of the Rebel.

'Prime the cannons and fire on my command,' shouted the Captin, then he followed the direction of the First Mate's gaze.

'Holy Smoke! Is that an angel?' cried the First Mate, pointing up at the vision of a lady, white petticoats billowing in the wind. The Captain was too astonished to speak. Sadie landed on the deck, and her momentum caused her to stumble forward into the First Mate's arms.

'Hello, Sailor!' she giggled.

Meanwhile, Oliver clutched onto the end of a rope suspended from the Rebel and swung towards the Albion's rigging. Nathan, having previously journeyed to Africa on the Rebel, was not at all phased by the sight of the airship and burst out laughing when Oliver's foot caught in the rigging, and he was left hanging upside down. Oliver, however, was not amused and yelled:

'Cut that blasted flag down. It's an enemy flag. They'll sink you. And get me down, damn you!"

It took a little while for Nathan to grasp the urgency of the situation, but then his crew sprang into action, and a seaman with a knife gripped between his teeth climbed swiftly up the rigging to free Oliver.

'I hope you are planning to cut the ropes that bind me and not aiming to remove my foot, dear boy,' remarked Oliver, regaining his usual civility.

On the Guardian, Sadie was trying to make the Captain believe her.

'Honestly, it's not a Confederate ship. They've been tricked!' The Captain's suspicions were evident in the expression on his face. He thought this was all some kind of ruse. Then a voice rang out from the crow's nest:

Captain. They have taken down the Confederate Flag and are now flying the British flag.

'Told you!' said Sadie triumphantly. 'Now, I've got to tell you about the submersible.'

'The what?'

'It's a ship that travels under the water.' A look of confusion and mistrust returned to the Captain's face, followed by one of alarm at the sight of the airship returning and seemingly on a collision course with his ship.

'Cor blimey, look at 'em go!' yelled Billy, peering out of the airship's door.

Jake was gratified to see his tadpoles swimming furiously and succeeding in keeping the net in a hammock shape. Charlotte was chasing down the dark shape, as it headed towards the oblivious Guardian.

'I don't think we are going to get there in time,' she shouted, 'I'm going as fast as I can.'

Inside the submersible, it was hard going.

'Faster! Let's get this over with,' shouted Ethan.

'I can't,' moaned Isaac. 'I can hardly breathe, and it's too hot in here.'

'We can surface and replenish the air once we have completed our mission. We are nearly there,' shouted Ethan.

In the end, the dwindling air supply was a crucial factor. It increased the fatigue felt by the crew, so the submersible slowed down considerably. Charlotte was on a collision course with the American Navy ship and was within a few seconds of slamming the Rebel into the Guardian, when she managed to guide the net below the submersible.

'That's it!' yelled Billy, 'Up, up, up. Quick as yer bleedin' well can!'

The airship struggled to gain height now that it was carrying a heavy metal submersible, and a collision seemed inevitable.

'I can't, she won't!' gasped Charlotte, and she did the only thing possible to save them. She slammed the controls hard to starboard and then back again, shifting the flightpath of the airship by a few feet. The Rebel soared between two of the Guardian's three masts, causing Sadie and the sailors to throw themselves on the deck to avoid the monstrous metal creature swinging towards them.

'That's what I were talkin' about,' said Sadie, getting to

her feet and smoothing down her petticoats. 'I reckon they have caught themselves a submersible.'

Charlotte slowed the Rebel down in an effort to stop the net swinging.

'Why don't they come out?' asked Billy. 'It can't be much fun in there.'

'They are probably too dizzy,' laughed Joshua, watching the net spinning below them.

'I wonder if they have enough air,' said Jake. 'I think we ought to go and check. Come on, Joshua.' They scrambled down the rope ladder to the net. The tadpoles were still whirring; their clockwork engines hadn't run down, but they were completely ineffective out of the water. Jake and Joshua struggled to weave their way through the tangled netting to reach the submersible. Joshua had brought a bag of tools with him. He rapped on the side of the craft with a wrench and listened for sounds from inside. Silence!

'The hatch will be locked from the inside,' shouted Jake, 'We have to find another way in.'

'Here!' Joshua had discovered a small porthole mounted near the front of the submersible. 'It's too small to get through.'

'Never mind. See if you can break the glass and let some air in,' said Jake.

Unfortunately, the combination of the thickness of the glass and the netting wrapped around them, conspired against Joshua. He couldn't find room to get enough backswing, and his wrench bounced harmlessly off the window. 'Let me try,' cried Jake. Jake had purposely fitted the hand he called the Toolkit. He activated the clockwork motor and extended the finger that transformed into a drill. Knowing there might be men who were suffocating inside made every second seem like an hour, but he was gratified to see shavings of glass spinning off the window and falling to the sea below. 'Is there a hammer and a nail in your bag, Joshua?' Joshua rooted around in the bag and found a nail. At the same time, Jake's drill bit plunged into the window. He had made a hole. Not enough to fully ventilate the submersible, but it was a start.

'No hammer. I could climb up to the gondola and get one.'

'No time. Fit the point of the nail into this hole and hit it with your wrench. While you are doing that, I'll drill another hole.' It took two more holes before they achieved a result. First, a crack appeared, joining the first two holes, then finally, after the third fissure, they were able to punch out a triangle of glass and could feel warm, stale air escaping from within.

It was dark inside. Jake thought he could see a crew member's limbs but could not see any movement. Joshua came to the opening and began to shout:

'Isaac! Isaac! Wake up!'

CHAPTER SEVEN

Charlotte kept the airship as stationary as possible, trying to stop the heavy load from swinging too violently. She watched Jake and Joshua with concern as they struggled to gain access to the submersible.

'Wot d'ya reckon that pointy bit is sticking out the front?' asked Billy.

'I've no idea,' replied Charlotte. 'No doubt Jake will want to investigate once they've freed the crew. 'Have you wound the clockwork motor up, Billy? We need all the power we can get.'

'Already dunnit. Cor blimey, where 'ave they come from?'

Two sailboats were racing across the waves below, heading back towards New York.

'My guess is that the leading one is from the Confederate ship, and the other is chasing it, either from the warship or from Nathan's ship, the Albion,' Charlotte replied.

Isaac was trying to get to sleep but couldn't get in a good position. The bed was too hard and his grandfather kept calling for him. It was time to get up and plant yams, but he would rather stay where he was and drift off to sleep again.

'Isaac! Isaac! Isaac!'

It was all very annoying, and he tried to reply; his mouth formed words, but no sound came out. Then he coughed and opened his eyes. For a few moments, he was confused. He wasn't lying in a hut in Africa after all.

'Isaac! Isaac! Isaac!' He realised that voice wasn't his grandfather's. It was Joshua! But what was he doing here, and where was this? Then his senses cleared, and he recognised the other crew members sprawled around him. He tried to cry out, but what emerged was more of a whimper. Encouraged, Joshua called again:

'Isaac! Isaac! Isaac! You have to open the hatch from the inside to escape. Open it, Isaac.'

Isaac made his way to the hatch, steeling himself to crawl over his fellow crew members. His head was throbbing and his movements were slow, but eventually he found himself clutching the large wheel mounted below the hatch. At first, he couldn't turn it, so he braced his legs against the sides of the hatch and heaved with all his might. With a squeal, the wheel began to move. A few inches at first, then more easily until the hatch gave way. He pushed, but he could only open it a crack. He felt cool, fresh air rush through the gap. He was exhausted and could do no more, but the weight of the hatch was shouldered by

Joshua, who opened it fully.

'Joshua…how…?'

'Not now. Later. Put this on.' Billy had lowered the rope with the harness fixed to the end, and Joshua now fastened it onto Isaac. On a signal from Jake, Billy hoisted Isaac up to the airship, confused and disorientated.

'I'll go in and see if anyone else is alive,' said Jake, 'There's not enough room in there for you, Joshua!' Jake lowered himself through the hatch. Meanwhile, Joshua stepped onto the rope ladder to get a better view of two sailboats passing directly below them.

Double Top was on the first boat and was furious that, after months of careful planning, everything had gone wrong. The Osprey's crew knew they had no choice but to wait to be boarded by the sailors from the Guardian. They certainly couldn't outrun it. Maybe they could plead innocence about the purpose of the submersible: something that would prove more straightforward if a suspected Confederate spy was not found onboard. That suited Double Top; he didn't want to face a firing squad, and he would be of more use to the cause if his role in the plot was kept secret, and he could melt back into the New York crowds. Maybe it was time to return south anyway. He had other business interests to look after.

Double Top looked back at the pursuing sailboat, which was gaining on them, and yelled at the skipper of his boat.

'Can't you go any faster?' He drew his pistol. When the sailboat was close enough, he would fire, but right now, as his boat bounced along the waves, he would surely miss. Frustrated, he looked up at the cause of all his grief: the airship. He fired a shot at it. The airship was a more prominent target and within range, but he would still be lucky to hit it from this distance and from aboard an ocean-tossed boat.

It was a lucky shot, indeed. Fortunately for Charlotte and Billy, Double Top's bullet did not hit the airship, but the consequences were still disastrous. The bullet hit the torpedo strapped to the front of the submersible, and with a thunderous crash, it exploded, setting fire to the net. Joshua, who was on the rope ladder, was swung aside by the force of the explosion and to his horror, he saw the submersible plunge through a hole in the burning netting and spin down to the sea below, hitting the waves with a mighty splash.

Jake had no idea what was happening. He heard an explosion and saw a flash of light funnelled down through the open escape hatch. The next thing he knew, he was spiralling downwards and bouncing against the sides of the submersible. Then he was jarred by the impact as it hit the water, throwing him against the back wall of the chamber. Water started to flood inside. It took Jake a few moments to orientate himself and realise that the submersible was upside down. Standing upright, he could breathe from an air pocket caught at the top of the compartment. Then he noticed that it wasn't completely pitch dark.

The explosion had caused a fissure along the weld of a panel, so whilst it meant daylight could filter in, Jake realised that air would seep out, and the water level inside would rise. It would not be long before the submersible sank. Disconcertingly, he was sharing the space with the other crew members who were floating face down. He hadn't been able to detect a pulse in any of them before the explosion, but now he was more concerned about his own survival. If the submersible sank with him still inside, that would be the end, so he first needed to get out of the craft.

Then he would face another major obstacle - he couldn't swim! Jake filled his lungs and dropped below the surface. He felt for the crankshaft and, hand over hand, he hauled himself along until he was before the escape hatch. He kicked out, grasped the ladder fixed to the side of the hatch, and pulled himself outside the submersible, but he was still underwater. He reached out, his metal hand clawing the sides of the submersible in order to get some kind of grip, and a moment before his breath ran out, he emerged gasping into the daylight. Ahead of him, Jake could see the Rebel turning in an arc to reach him. However, the submersible was only an inch above the waves, air bubbles streaming out of the wounds in its sides. The airship wasn't going to reach him in time as the submersible was now sinking fast. He thrashed about, but now he began to take in gulps of seawater. Having a heavy metal hand didn't help. He contemplated whether to unscrew it but thought, 'What's the point? I can't swim with it or without it!' Jake's head sank below the waves. 'Aren't I supposed to see my whole life flashing before me? It hasn't been a very long life, so death should come quickly.' Then, a hand clutched his collar and yanked him upwards. Jake surfaced, spluttering. He couldn't see who had rescued him but he recognised the voice.

'Jake, I'm surprised at you!' scolded Oliver with good humour,' You should take more care! The saltwater won't be any good for your shiny metal hand.'

A short while later, Jake and Oliver were back on the Rebel. Oliver gazed out the window at the yacht on which he had been sailing and which was now returning to the Albion.

'It's a pity,' he murmured.

'A pity 'cause you bloomin' well nearly caught the

blighter?' asked Billy.

'No, I meant a pity that I'm going to miss the party. Nathan was already getting the rum out for a visit by the American Navy. Sadie is going to have all the fun. Still, we have work to do. Full speed ahead, Charlotte! Despite Double Top's head start, we should still get to New York before him.'

'Here we are, the New York Municipal Police headquarters,' said Oliver, leaping up the steps. Jake and Joshua followed him. Charlotte and Billy had returned to Trinity Church to tether the Rebel to the spire.

The desk sergeant looked up from the newspaper he was reading and smiled quizzically at the three men before him.

'There's a criminal on the loose,' burst out Jake. 'He's responsible for the deaths of five men, but it could have been much worse.'

'He's a Confederate spy,' added Joshua.

'Is that right? There's been a lot of talk about Confederates lately. Me? I think they're just stories to frighten the kids, like the bogeyman, to stop them from getting into mischief.' The policeman picked up a pipe resting on the desk and drew heavily on it, enveloping himself in a cloud of smoke. 'Ah! That's better. I thought I had let it go out.'

'Please, you must hurry. He'll be back in New York soon,' urged Jake.

'And where has this criminal, as you say, been carrying out his murderous activities?'

'At sea!'

'So not within the City limits. I think this is out of our

jurisdiction,' replied the sergeant.

'But they were New York boys killed in the submersible.'

'And what in God's name is a sub-mercybill?'

'It's a ship that travels underwater,' replied Jake.

'Is that right? Next thing you'll be telling me about is ships that fly in the air,' laughed the policeman.

'Well, as it happens...' started Jake, but Oliver put a warning hand on Jake's arm to silence him.

'We're wasting time,' Oliver said, 'We know where his hotel is, and we know his name. They call him Double Top.'

'Ah! Double Top. I know him!' cried the policeman excitedly, 'He's no Confederate. Oh, he's a grand fellow! He'll always get the first round in.'

'We have to go,' said Oliver to his companions. As they left the building, they heard the serjeant singing:

'In Dublin's fair city

Where the girls are so pretty

I first set my eyes on sweet Molly Malone...'

Ten minutes later, they were in sight of the hotel.

'Look!' said Joshua, pointing to two blue-uniformed men chatting on the street corner 'More policemen!'

'I do believe they are from the other New York police force, the Metropolitans,' said Oliver. 'Let's see if we can get a better response from them.'

In the event, it didn't take long to persuade them. As soon as they mentioned Double Top's name, one of the policemen replied:

'I know him. I've seen him buttering up those Irish Municipals. We used to be Natives.'

'They don't look like they are Indians,' whispered Jake to Oliver.

'No, the Natives are one of the local gangs - all-American boys who detest immigrants.'

'There he is,' called Joshua, 'I see him, coming from that side street.'

'Quicken your pace, but stay calm,' said a policeman, 'He won't be expecting us to grab him.'

'What! Take your hands off me!' growled Double Top as policemen grabbed either arm.

'That's him!' cried Joshua. Double Top studied Joshua for a moment, then remembering meeting him on the dockside with Isaac, he said:

'I know you!'

'And I know you for what you are,' replied Joshua, his lip curling as he stood face to face with his old enemy.

'Come on, boys!' This time, the shout emanated from three policemen racing along the street. Jake was just thinking they had the matter under control when, to his surprise, the new arrivals withdrew truncheons and started beating the first two constables about the head. Soon, a vicious fight was in progress between the Metropolitan and the Municipal police officers. In the turmoil, they had all forgotten about Double Top, until Joshua saw their adversary sidling away.

'No!' he yelled and chased after him, followed by Oliver and Jake, leaving the lawmen brawling in the middle of the street. Double Top, seeing Joshua bearing down on him, took flight and dodged into a narrow alleyway. Then he realised that Joshua would catch him if he continued to run, so he halted, holding out one hand in resignation.

'Alright, you win,' he said as Joshua slowed down to a walking pace with Oliver and Jake not far behind. Then, too late, Joshua saw Double Top was holding a pistol. As the report from the gun rang out, Joshua flung himself to one side.

'Agh!' Joshua felt the pain from the bullet tearing into his thigh and rolled over several times before coming to rest on his back in the dirt and grime. Oliver and Jake ran to attend to him, while Double Top vanished into the shadows.

Oliver ripped open Joshua's trousers where the bullet had passed through.

'You are lucky. It looks as though the bullet has entered. It's not lodged inside your leg.'

'I would have felt luckier if it had missed me altogether,' replied Joshua with a grimace.

'We'll get you back to our hotel and bandage you up. After you've rested awhile you'll be fine!' said Oliver.

'Do you think Double Top will return to his hotel?' asked Jake.

'No, I doubt he will have the audacity to do that. He will have recognised me and remembered that he took me there,' replied Oliver.

'If you can manage Joshua on your own, I could sneak into his room and see if he has left anything useful to help us track him down,' said Jake. 'I presume you want to find him.'

'Hell, yeah!' replied Joshua.

'And a "hell, yeah" from me too!' replied Oliver, 'Jake, give me a hand to get Joshua to the street, and we'll hail one of those rickshaws that operate all over New York since the horses died. It's one of the advantages of living in a city with a thriving Chinese quarter.'

DAVE JOHNSON

CHAPTER EIGHT

It wasn't in Jake's nature to be hasty. That is, if you discount the action that led to him becoming one of the Rebel Runaways in the first place when he hit Hastings on the back of the head. Jake was waiting outside the hotel when a family carrying cases arrived. Then, knowing the receptionist would be busy allocating them rooms, he walked calmly to the staircase as though he was already a guest. Oliver had described where Double Top's room was, and Jake found it with no difficulty. Getting inside was just as easy. Jake was still wearing his 'toolkit' hand, unharmed by its dip in the ocean. He had prepared for just this kind of occasion when he designed it, and now pressed a button that engaged the tool for picking locks. He inserted it into the keyhole, and after a gentle flick of his wrist, he swiftly stepped through the door, locking it behind him.

The first thing that Jake noticed was a trunk on the bed packed with clothes. 'So Double Top is already set to leave New York, anyway,' he thought. Jake searched methodically through the trunk. He didn't find anything useful, and although it would have been quicker to leave all the clothes scattered on the bed, that wasn't his way, and he replaced everything as he had found it.

He noticed an envelope on the bedside table that was addressed and ready to post. He studied the address and lodged it in his memory; he wouldn't forget it but, thinking that the letter's contents might be interesting, he placed it in his pocket. Then he moved on to investigate a safe that Oliver had told him about, in which Double Top had kept the bond that Oliver purchased. Even if Oliver had noticed the combination, he would have been too drunk to remember it! Jake listened intently as he turned the dials on the safe, hoping to hear a click that would reveal he had the correct number. What he heard instead was the sound of a key turning in the door lock. For a moment, Jake froze; someone was coming into the room. If it was a cleaner, Jake wouldn't be able to explain his presence; if it was Double Top, the situation would be far worse; Double Top had a gun! There were only three places to hide: under the bed, in the wardrobe or in the bathroom. Jake chose the latter - he didn't want to get trapped in a cramped space where he couldn't defend himself. The bathroom door had been open when he arrived, so he quickly slipped behind it, held his breath, and waited. To his horror, Jake saw Double Top's reflection in the bathroom mirror. If he were to look in the mirror, he would see Jake. Jake crouched down so he was out of sight. He heard the trunk being closed and dragged off the bed. Then he heard Double Top grunt in annoyance followed by the sound of furniture being moved and the wardrobe door slamming. Finally, the trunk was hauled across the floorboards before the room door banged shut and Double Top was gone.

Jake crept out into the room. Double Top had moved the bed and opened the wardrobe door. Jake waited for a few moments before leaving the room. Near the bottom of the stairs, he paused at the sound of Double Top shouting angrily at the receptionist.

'How many times do I have to tell you? The letter was definitely in that room, ready to be posted.'

'It's a mystery, Sir. You say the room was locked. I can assure you that our staff have not been in there. I knew you were leaving today, so I did not schedule the room to be cleaned until after you had left. Did the letter contain anything valuable, Sir?'

'No! It's just a nuisance having to write it again. I'm not happy, I tell you. This day is going from bad to worse.'

'Your rickshaw is here, Sir. I'll take your trunk.'

Once Double Top had gone, Jake emerged. The receptionist looked quizzically at him. Unfazed, Jake strode towards him with a smile.

'Excuse me; I am looking for one of your guests, Double Top. I've just been up to his room, but he doesn't appear to be in.'

'I'm sorry, Sir. You've just missed him. He's on his way to the railway station.'

Joshua was lying in bed with his heavily bandaged leg outstretched. The Rebel Runaways gathered around him to hear Jake recount his attempt to track Double Top.

'Then the trail went cold,' said Jake with a shrug. 'I

ran up and down platforms and through carriages, leaping off just as trains were about to depart, but with no luck. Double Top had a head start as he had travelled by rickshaw while I was on foot, so his train had probably gone before I arrived. A porter told me a train bound for Washington had just left. I'm guessing Double Top will be heading South, so maybe he was on that one. All we have is this,' he said, taking Double Top's envelope from his pocket and placing it on the table. Where is Little Ridge, Georgia, anyway? I really must spend some time studying a map!'

'I've never heard of Little Ridge,' said Joshua, 'But Georgia is in the South. It's slave country down there.'

'Double Top addressed this letter to "Juniper Farm", and it says inside that he is planning to visit it at the end of the month to carry out a stocktake,' said Charlotte.

'Excellent!' cried Oliver, 'You will be fit enough to travel by then, Joshua. Double Top hasn't seen the last of the Rebel Runaways!'

'I'm done with New York,' said Isaac, sitting on the end of Joshua's bed.

'So what are you going to do? Where are you going to go?' asked Joshua.

'I don't know exactly where I'm going, but I've joined the army. They reckon there's gonna be a draft anyway, so I reckon if I enlist before then, I might get treated better.'

'You know people are going to be shooting at you?'

'Well, that's better than them trying to blow me up in a tube under the water. I've got a score to settle with them Confederates, so I might as well get paid and fed while I'm doing it.'

'Good luck, Isaac. If you ever want to write me a letter, send it to this hotel. They will keep it for me.'

'I'll do that. I was always pretty good at writin', but I never had anything to write about. Maybe that's all gonna change! Anyway, I'd best be going. My ship sails in a couple of hours. We're going down to Washington for training. Thank Jake and all the others again for saving my life. I'll try not to lose it on the battlefield.'

'Why don't we go for a little promenade?' Sadie asked Charlotte, 'It's going to take a few days before Joshua is fit to travel, so we may as well explore New York. I've heard that Broadway is the street to be seen in.'

'Excellent idea, let's show them what a Rebel Runaway looks like! Is anyone else coming?'

'No, I want to strip down and clean my Toolkit hand in case the dip in the ocean did any damage,' replied Jake.

'Nah!' said Billy, shaking his head, 'I promised I'd give 'em some 'elp in the kitchen. Even though there's bleedin' loads o' people outta work, they've been findin' it difficult to get reliable staff. And yer can count Oliver out coz he's out fer the count! Ee's 'aving a feather and flip,'

'A what?' asked Charlotte.

'A feather and flip - kip! Oliver is sleepin' off a right 'orrible 'angover, so 'e won't be joinin' yer. Nuffin' to worry 'bout. Yer big gals now. Yer can manage without us 'oldin' yer 'and.'

"Tha cheeky little lad!' cried Sadie. She darted at Billy and tried to box him around the ears, but he was far too quick for her and leapt out of the way.

Thirty minutes later, Sadie and Charlotte had joined New York's fashionable set strolling down Broadway.

'The dress styles are different here,' commented Charlotte. 'Altogether less fussy than the fashions on Bond Street in London.'

'They are still very different from our clothes,' laughed Sadie. 'I love it when people stop and stare. So, now we are in downtown Manhattan, shall we call in at the shop that Genevieve told us about? What was it called, and what was the name of the French one she had visited?'

'The shop in Paris is called Le Bon Marché. I've never visited a store divided into departments as she described in her letter. Apparently, this New York one, A.T. Stewart's, is a huge shop too! It's on Broadway; they call it the Marble Palace.'

'That was certainly food for thought,' said Charlotte as they emerged from A.T. Stewart's an hour later, 'I've never seen so many products for sale under one roof.'

'Yes, but what is really interesting is all the ready-to-wear clothes on sale. Happen goin' to a couturier will soon be a thing o' th' past,' commented Sadie.

'I think the rich are always going to want a personal service, but are they the people we want to sell our clothes to?' asked Charlotte.

'I don't reckon that posh folk are likely to wear corsets or fancy waistcoats on the outside of their frocks with lots of petticoats and high lace-up leather boots, not to mention wearing bowler hats decorated with flying goggles!' laughed Sadie.

'What's going on down there?' asked Charlotte. They turned off Broadway into a side street. Charlotte pointed to a small crowd gathered before a man standing behind a folding table.

'Come on, let's take a look. I've got my Glove wi' me in case things get a bit lairy,' said Sadie.

When the girls got closer, they could see that the man was performing a card trick.

'All you've got to do is find the lady. I've got a Queen, a King and a Jack,' he said, showing each of the three cards in turn, 'I'll put them on the table, one, two, three. Where's the lady? Here, of course,' he said, flipping over a card to reveal the Queen. 'I'll do it again; here's the Queen, here's the King and here's the Jack. I'll lay them down. One, two, three. Where is she?' A man reached over and placed a coin on one of the cards.

'She's there!'

'Quite right, Sir. You've won a dime. If only you had bet a dollar, you would have won a dollar! You know me; I'm Honest John; I always pay my dues.'

'I've got a dollar,' shouted another man, 'Do it again.' Honest John showed the audience the three cards, placed them on the table and mixed up the order. The gambler put down his dollar on the card in the centre.

'It's not my lucky day,' complained Honest John, handing the man his winnings. 'How about you, young lady? You've got a lucky face.'

'This is all the money I have,' said the girl, holding up a quarter. She had a soft Irish accent and her clothes were faded and worn.

'Well, wouldn't it be better to have fifty cents than twenty-five, Miss? Here they are, Queen, King, Jack. A quick shuffle around, and now, where's the lady?' The young girl started to reach out with her money, but Sadie caught her arm.

'I can spare a quarter,' said Sadie to the girl, 'I'll put the money down. If I win, I'll share it with you. Just tell me where to put it.'

'Very generous of you, Madam,' said Honest John.

'It's there,' said the young girl confidently, pointing to the centre card. Sadie fished in her purse and placed a quarter on the table.

'Is she there? Oh, bad luck this time, Madam,' said John as he flipped over a King. The girl gasped in surprise:

'I was sure it was there. I would have lost all my money, and now I've lost yours for you!'

'Never mind,' said Sadie. It was only a quarter. Can I have another go?' she asked brightly.

'Certainly. You know me; I'm Honest John; I always pay my dues.'

'No matter how many times you say it,' thought Charlotte, 'You are never going to convince me that you are honest!'

'Here they are, your friends and mine: Queen, King, Jack.' Honest John dealt out the cards again, shuffled them around, and it was clear to Charlotte that the Queen was in the centre.

'Does it matter how much money I put down?' asked Sadie innocently.

'No, no. You are at liberty to win as much as you like.'

'In that case,' she said, 'I have a Double Eagle,' and put a twenty-dollar gold coin on the card to her left. Now it was Charlotte's turn to gasp. Not only was it a lot of money, but she was convinced that Sadie had placed her bet on the wrong card. When she looked at Honest John, she saw that he was wide-eyed in surprise.

'I'm sorry but…' he began and reached out for the card but snatched his hand away as a metal dart pinned the card to the table. Sadie, wearing her Glove on her right hand, reached with her left and folded back the corner of the card she had pierced. It was a Queen.

'You said there was no limit,' she said firmly.

'But... that's a lot of money!'

'Empty your purse on the table.' With a trembling hand and keeping an eye on Sadie's dart-firing glove, Honest John tipped the contents of a leather purse onto the table. Sadie quickly examined the coins. 'I reckon that's about seventeen dollars. And your accomplice - he's got two dollars.' The man who had earlier won at the trick reached into his pocket and took out two coins. 'And you, I'll have your two dimes,' she said to the other 'lucky' winner. 'That will have to do. I shan't be lending you the money to buy a new deck of cards, mind,' and she fired a dart that pinned the rest of the pack to the table. 'I'll take my quarter and my Double Eagle back,' she said, picking up the coins, 'And you, my young friend,' said Sadie, turning to the young Irish girl, 'Pick up the rest of the money and put it in your purse.'

The astonished girl did as she was told. Then, linking her arm, Sadie said, 'And now, you honest gentlemen, it's time we took our leave.' Sadie, Charlotte and the young girl walked away from the murmuring crowd. 'We'll walk you home, just in case they decide to follow you to steal the money. What's your name?'

'It's Ellen; who are you? You look so different! Are you guardian angels?' asked Ellen.

'I'm certainly no angel, love. But that's a long story! I'm Sadie.'

'And I'm Charlotte. We'll tell you our story, and you can tell us yours over an ice cream.'

Twenty minutes later, they were sitting at the counter in an ice cream parlour.

'I've never eaten anything so delicious,' enthused Ellen.

'It's better than we have in London,' said Sadie.

'Talk about sleight of hand, Sadie,' laughed Charlotte,

'I didn't notice that you had put your Glove on! Tell me, how did you know where the Queen was?'

'As you know, I worked at Madame Boo-Boo's,' said Sadie, 'And that's not a story for your delicate ears,' she said with a sideways glance towards Ellen, 'There was a client called Harry the Ace, and he would entertain all the girls with card tricks. As you now realise, Honest John had accomplices who appeared to be winning and were betting on the same card you would. They were just there to sucker you in. Honest John made a subtle change to his technique as soon as real money was bet. You would have got so used to him dealing the Queen first that you wouldn't notice that he had dealt from the bottom, and you would be chasing the wrong card. So I definitely knew which one it wasn't - the obvious one - and I guessed it would be on his right, as he was right-handed. I could have been wrong, but I wasn't.'

'What are you going to spend your winnings on, Ellen?' asked Charlotte.

'Are you sure I can keep it? I owe so much rent, and I haven't been able to find a job. The landlord says there are other ways I can pay him back, but he's not a nice man.'

'That, my girl, will not be happening!' promised Sadie.

Sadie and Charlotte had spoken to Oliver, and now Oliver was talking with the hotel manager.

'I've not met her myself, but I am assured that Ellen is an honest, clean-living girl, not long over from Dublin. She has faced some hard times recently. She came over to stay with her Aunt only to find her already dead from smallpox.'

'Well, I'm not sure...'

'Billy tells me you're short-staffed in the kitchen. He's

not going to be around much longer to help you because it won't be long before Joshua is fit to travel, and then we will all be leaving.'

'Well, that's true, but...'

'I'll tell you what. How about if I pay her wages for the first two months?'

'Well, now that...'

'On condition that you give her a room here in the hotel. A respectable young girl like her shouldn't be living down in the Five Points.'

'Yes, I suppose...'

'Shake on it!' The two men shook hands, and the precarious nature of Ellen's existence in New York was no more. She had a future!

DAVE JOHNSON

CHAPTER NINE

'I notice that white officer who gave us the orders ain't getting on this end of the train,' commented Isaac.

'Hush your mouth now, city boy,' rebuked the Sergeant, 'If you wanna survive in this here army, you better learn to keep your mouth shut or else you are gonna have your card marked, and when you've finished digging out the latrines you're gonna be marching in the front line with every crazy grayback there is shootin' at you.'

'Well, I was just noticing that all the white men who enlisted are at the front of the train, and all the black men are at the back. Shoot! Even the pigs are further up the train than we are. Betcha, when this train gets movin', we gonna be downwind of all that pork.'

'I'm telling you. Keep your noticin' to yourself. It's not

just about you no more. To survive, we gotta act as a team. If they think you're a troublemaker with all your bellyaching, then we might all suffer the consequences. What's your name?

'It's Isaac Thompson,'

'Ain't you forgetting something?'

'I haven't got a middle name,' replied Isaac, puzzled. The Sergeant burst out laughing:

'God help us turn you all into soldiers! Let me remind you - you don't have a blue uniform, you haven't got a gun, and even if you had one, you probably wouldn't know how to shoot it, and you most definitely haven't got any horse sense, but that don't matter cause we ain't got no horses no more, but you are in the army now. That means I can call you dumbass if I want, but you have to call me Sir or Sergeant.'

'Yes, Sir'

'Those men at the front of the train are gonna get to Virginia a few seconds before you, but what they gonna do with all that extra time? Nothing! Because they gonna be waitin' for you!'

'Now that you put it that way, the idea of white men having to wait until I'm good and ready, is a whole different situation. I'm liking the sound of that!' smiled Isaac.

'Now boys, try and get some shut-eye. Sleep might be in short supply from now on,' said the Sergeant.

A low-lying mist swirled around the trees in the Virginian forest as the early morning sun filtered through the canopy. The dawn chorus echoed around the pines, gradually swallowed by the sound of the approaching steam train. Onboard, Isaac and his companions were stretched out on the bare boards of the goods carriage, and all were fast asleep. The rhythm of their breathing kept time with the clickity-clack of the iron wheels on the track, then suddenly all were shocked awake by of an explosion and the sound of metal screeching on metal and men screaming in the half-light as the carriage slowly slid to a halt.

'What's happening?' shouted Isaac in alarm. The Sergeant was already peering out of the window and was shocked by what he saw. Their carriage was the only one untouched - the others lay twisted and broken on the track. To his horror, he saw a line of men, muskets readied. Their grey uniforms took shape against the grey mist of the forest as they approached the train.

'It's an ambush!' cried the Sergeant. He quickly took stock of the situation. He was the only trained man in a bunch of raw recruits with only one gun between them. 'Quiet!' he shouted, sensing panic starting to set in. 'If we stay, we're gonna get killed. We have to leave now - quietly and quickly - out of the back of the carriage, and head into the woods on our right. The Johnny Rebs won't see us if we hurry. Follow me!' As he slid the door back and leapt down from the carriage, the air was filled with the sound of gunfire, which strengthened the incentive for a swift exodus from the train. Once the party had been swallowed up by the forest, the Sergeant gestured to the men to stop and gather around him. The distant gunfire had ceased, to be replaced by hoots of laughter from the victorious Confederate soldiers.

'I don't know where we are. All I know is that the train was taking us to where we needed to go, so we should follow the route of the railroad tracks. We'll stay in the forest for a while until we are sure we are out of sight, and then we will get back to the railroad line, where the going will be quicker and easier.'

Thirty minutes later, the men were walking in single file, along the railway tracks. They walked in silence, not because they had been ordered to, but because the violent awakening had shocked them into realising that danger might be their constant companion from now on. Suddenly, the Sergeant stopped and held up his hand to bring the men to a halt. He crept forward to inspect the mound piled on the railroad tracks.

'Dynamite!' he whispered. Gesturing to the men to follow him, he stepped well clear of the explosives and began to run parallel to the railway track. After a few minutes, he slowed down and stepped back into the forest to talk to his exhausted men.

'Gather round. What we have just seen is another ambush in the making. I saw a detonator line leading into the woods, which means there are probably more soldiers hiding, waiting to attack another train. Obviously, a train ain't gonna come from behind us. The train we were riding is blocking the way, so they must be expecting a train from the South. We have to warn any train coming this way.' The Sergeant reached up into a tree and broke off a branch. Then he unbuttoned his blue tunic, took off his shirt, and tied it to the branch to make a flag. Several other men followed suit. Then they all returned to the railroad tracks to continue the journey.

An hour later, one of the men dropped to the ground and put his ear to the track.

'It's vibrating,' he shouted, 'There's a train a-coming!'

'You men with the flags - spread yourself along the track and be prepared to jump out of the way. It may not be inclined to stop. I'll go further back,' yelled the Sergeant.

On the train, the Engineer was getting up a head of steam. The Fireman had been working hard, shovelling coal into the firebox.

'Little and often, little and often,' the Fireman chanted.

'Well, I'll be damned, there's negroes on the track,' yelled the Engineer giving a long blast on the whistle.

'We ain't letting them on, but you had better slow down. We'll have to write a report if we kill any of 'em,' the Conductor pointed out, and he shouted to the brakeman, 'Charlie! Stop the train.'

'Well, I'll be...! Thisun's a soldier.' The train screeched to a halt a few inches away from the Sergeant, who steadfastly refused to budge. Eventually, the rest of the soldiers came racing to join him. Once he was satisfied that there was a human barrier to prevent the train from moving, the Sergeant left his position to explain the situation to the Engineer. It seemed a long while before the Engineer lowered the rifle aimed at the Sergeant's head.

Ten minutes later, the passengers in Coach A were astonished to see first the Conductor and then the Sergeant and his men climb aboard the train.

'Don't be alarmed, folks,' the Conductor shouted to the passengers, 'But we are going to have to go back.' Up until then, the passengers had been grumbling about the train stopping and about seeing the negroes outside, but as the train jolted into reverse and slowly began to travel back the way they had come, the discontent turned to anger, and some shouted insulting comments. Isaac couldn't contain his feelings and stepped further into the carriage.

'We may look like a bunch of raggedy negroes to you,' he shouted, 'But let me tell you this - we have all enlisted in the Union army and are prepared to die for our country.

Let me repeat that - OUR country - and I'll tell you another thing: if it weren't for the leadership of our brave Sergeant here, we would all be dead, and so would you because there's a Confederate ambush waiting for you down the line.' A young girl stood up.

'You can have my seat,' she said, 'I'll see if I can find another further down the train. If not, I'm happy to stand. Thank you for saving my life.' One by one, the passengers stood up and offered their seats. The last to sit down were the Sergeant and Isaac.

'Well said, soldier,' said the Sergeant, 'What's your name again?'

'It's Isaac, Sir.'

'Well said, Isaac, my name is Luke Taylor.'

It was midday when the train arrived, and the Engineer and the Stationmaster stood on the platform and watched as the passengers formed a guard of honour. Two lines of people clapped as the black soldiers proudly marched between them.

'What I don't understand is, what would the Confederates gain by killing a load of civilians?' asked the Engineer.

'Not a thing,' replied the Stationmaster. 'They were waiting to blow up a troop train. They weren't to know that the troop train had engine problems and that we switched around the schedule, so you ended up going ahead of them.'

'That explains it,' nodded the Engineer, 'I know there's a lot of support for the Southern cause in these parts, and blowing us up would have harmed that support.'

'It would have harmed you too,' chuckled the Stationmaster. 'I've got a bottle of whisky in the office. Let's toast your lucky escape.'

One Month Later

'Hey Luke, can I ask you a question?'

'I told you, Isaac, you gotta call me Sergeant or Sir when we are on duty.'

'But it's the middle of the night, everyone else is asleep, and this sentry post is right on the edge of the camp, so who's gonna hear me?' protested Isaac.

'It don't matter. Rules is rules. What do you want to ask me?'

'I was just wondrin' if you were married.'

'Nope.'

'You got a sweetheart waiting for you?'

'Well...'

'You have, haven't you? Do you have any children?'

'Hell, no!' We only kissed once.'

'Where does she live?'

'You ask a lot of questions, don't you? She's in Washington. She's called Jessy, and she's a maid working for Major Bannock's wife. How about you? Have you got a girl?'

'No, I've got no one. No mother, no father, no brothers or sisters. Just me. Have you got brothers and sisters, Sergeant?'

'More questions! Yes, I have a sister, but I don't rightly know if she's alive or dead because I haven't seen her since we were both sold into slavery.

'Maybe you should ask some of the other soldiers if they have seen her. There are men from all over the country. Maybe one of them has seen her,' suggested Isaac.

'The problem is, I don't know what name the slave

traders gave her. I only know her African name, which is Amara.'

'That's a sweet name.'

'It means 'Grace'.'

'So what's your African name, Sir? I don't got one because I was born in America.'

'It's Kambi.'

'Well how about that! That was my grandfather's name. Maybe we are related!'

'All black people are brothers,' smiled Luke.

Just then, a shot rang out, and a bullet thudded into the log that they were sitting on. Luke and Isaac scrambled to safety as two more bullets hit a tree behind them. There was a pause, and Luke peeked over the top of the log.

'I can't see anyone,' he whispered. As he dropped back down, another shot whistled over his head, followed by two more. 'I reckon there are three of them, and, by the sound of it, they've got muskets, not repeating rifles.'

'Do we go after them?' asked Isaac.

'No, you'll have plenty of other opportunities to be a hero. Right now, we are on guard, and if we head into the woods and get ourselves killed, there won't be anyone guarding the camp. Give me your hat.' Puzzled, Isaac did as he was told. Luke reached for a branch lying on the ground and perched the hat on top of it. Then he slowly raised it so the hat was just in view of the snipers. Three shots came in quick succession, and the hat was sent spinning away.

'My hat!' cried Isaac indignantly, but Luke ignored him, sprang up and shouldered his rifle.

'Quick, return their fire while they are reloading.' He fired his musket, then dropped back down again, located his powder and musket ball and swiftly started to reload his musket.

'I can't see 'em,' shouted Isaac.

'It don't matter, just shoot and get down.' Isaac shot blindly into the trees and dived back behind the tree trunk. A second later, another bullet whizzed by. Luke reached for Isaac's hat to tempt the other two snipers to fire. It worked again, and two shots rang out; once again, Isaac's hat was sent tumbling along the ground, pierced by another bullet hole.

'How come it's my hat getting shot to bits?' complained Isaac.

'You gotta learn to reload quicker, boy. Damn! They are fast; they're easily firing three shots a minute,' said Luke as he fired again. 'Crawl along to the end of the log and shoot from there. I'll go to the other end. We ain't expecting to hit them. We's just reminding them we're still here whilst reinforcements come from the camp.' Luke gave a short laugh as he scrambled to the far end of the log, 'I s'pose that's what they are doing too, reminding us that they are near. Damn! Those Johnny Rebs are gettin' mighty cheeky!' Just then, a bugle sounded from the camp. 'Keep your head down. Don't do anything stupid.' The bugle call came again, and a lone voice in the woods sang out in response:

I wish I was in the land of cotton, old times there are not forgotten,

Look away, look away, look away, Dixie Land.' Then all was silent.

'That's it. The excitement's over. Them graybacks are just going to slip away into the night,' said Luke. 'In the old days, we would have sent the cavalry after them, but now the cavalry ain't got no horses; they don't stand a chance of catching them.'

'Hell! Would you look at this?' complained Isaac,

poking his fingers through the holes in his hat.
    'Wear it with pride, son. It means you've seen action.'

CHAPTER TEN

'That's the bloomin' motor all wound up good and proper, and I've made a load of sandwiches so we can 'ave a right old nosh-up at lunchtime. I might as well 'ave meself a little kip 'cause there's nuffing else to do,' yawned Billy.

'Now that we've travelled south, the sky has gone a funny shade of yellow,' observed Sadie as she joined Charlotte at the helm.

'I know, it's as though it's sucked up all the colour from the ground. Is Oliver awake? There's a strong wind from the east and I'm struggling to keep us flying in a straight line. I wonder if he has experienced conditions like these before.' A few minutes later, having been woken from his slumbers, Oliver joined them at the helm.

'Hmm!' I don't like the look of this,' he muttered, 'It

looks like there's some bad weather on the way.'

'Can we outrun it?' asked Charlotte.

'Not if there's a tornado coming our way. At its slowest, it might be travelling at fifty miles an hour, but if it's a nasty, bad-tempered one, the wind speed might be over two hundred miles an hour.'

'Could we tether the Rebel and ride it out?' asked Charlotte.

'I think that would be sensible,' said Oliver. Jake and Joshua had joined them at the helm - Jake pointed to a lone, blackened tree below. Only the trunk and major boughs remained, stretching up to the sky as though in a plea for mercy.

'How about that tree?' asked Jake, 'It looks like it's been struck by lightning in the past. There aren't many others to choose from. Joshua could fire a harpoon with a cable attached, and we could tie the Rebel up to it.'

'I think that's our best option,' agreed Oliver, 'How is your wound, Joshua? Have you healed enough to do this? I could have a go, but you are an experienced shot with the Gauntlet.'

'I will be alright if I can lie on the deck and shoot out of the door,' replied Joshua. 'I don't fancy dangling on the end of a rope just yet. The bullet hole might open up.'

Charlotte began manoeuvring the Rebel level with the tree. Normally, she would have managed this easily, but the strength of the wind meant that it took all her might to hold the wheel steady.

'I can help,' said Oliver, reaching for the wheel.

'Don't you dare! I can manage!' snapped Charlotte. Inwardly, though, she wasn't certain she could cope unaided. Oliver took a few steps back, happy to let Charlotte handle the Rebel alone but close enough to step in if needed.

'You are doing really well,' soothed Sadie as Charlotte wrestled with the controls, powering the engine to full throttle to fight against the headwind.

'Just a few feet more,' urged Jake, 'That's it, Charlotte; hold the Rebel there if you can. Now, Joshua, fire!' Joshua pulled the trigger, and his harpoon shot through the sky and thudded into the tree trunk.

'Keep her steady!' shouted Oliver, 'I'll tie the other end of the rope to the docking ring. Hold on to my feet, someone.' Jake obliged, and Oliver leant out of the gondola's door to secure the cable to a ring mounted below it.

'Phew! It's a good job you were holding on to me. That's quite some wind out there. I could easily have been blown away,' he gasped as he scrambled back inside and fastened the door. 'Charlotte, you must ease back on the controls very slowly so the Rebel finds her natural place in the wind. I'm afraid it won't be a particularly comfortable and smooth experience for a while. We'll just have to ride it out.'

Over the next twenty minutes, the airship swayed and dipped as it was buffeted by the wind. Sadie's every instinct screamed at her to screw her eyes shut and curl up into a ball, but she forced herself to stay by Charlotte's side. There was little her friend could do to steady the Rebel, but she didn't want to abandon the helm and leave the wheel spinning uncontrollably. Oliver stared steadfastly out of the cabin window.

'Oh, my God! Oh no!' he gasped.

'What is it?' screamed Sadie, almost hysterical by now. Oliver pointed:

'It's a twister, and it's heading our way!' Ahead, a

furiously rotating column of dust, water droplets and debris sucked up from the ground, snaked across the landscape. It stretched to the clouds and made a frightening roaring sound as it approached.

'Hold on to something!' shouted Oliver. 'Tie yourself to the Rebel if you can.'

Oliver and Joshua used their belts to strap themselves to their seats. Jake clamped his metal hand to the gondola's frame, confident it would hold him securely.

'I can't leave the wheel,' cried Charlotte. Now Sadie sprang into action and reached for a coil of rope, which she tied into a lasso, laying the loop at Charlotte's feet.

'Step into it,' she commanded, and then she did likewise and pulled it up to waist height. She tightened it until they were squeezed together and then fastened the other end to the helm. Sadie wrapped her arms around Charlotte's midriff and held on; only then did she let herself shut her eyes.

By now, the tornado was louder than a freight train, and the airship began to buck violently, but worse was to come. As the twister reached the Rebel, the airship was caught up in its vortex, spinning faster and faster.

'The tree, the tree!' screamed Sadie. From their vantage point at the helm, only she and Charlotte could see that the tornado had uprooted the tree they had been secured to, and it had joined them to spin around the twisting column.

'What's happened?' shouted Oliver, reacting to the alarm in Sadie's voice and sensing that the airship was climbing higher and higher.

'It's the tree! The twister has pulled it out of the ground!' Oliver realised instantly that the situation was now even more dangerous. The Rebel could be dashed to bits if it collided with the tree. Oliver undid the belt securing himself to his seat, and, with great difficulty, he crawled across the deck, at times being tossed up into the air, until at last he reached the winch. He strapped himself into the harness at the end of the rope and called to Jake:

'Pass me a knife, and can you operate the winch for me?' Now that the wind was roaring all around them, it wouldn't be safe for Oliver to lean out of the gondola held only by his feet, as before. Jake crawled and rolled across the deck. He handed Oliver a sharp knife, clipped himself to the base of the winch, and gave a nod. Oliver took a deep breath to steel himself and turned the door handle. Immediately, the wind wrenched it from his hand. The tornado's force howled around the gondola as Oliver reached outside, sending charts and notebooks flying in all directions. Suddenly, the wind caught Oliver, and he careered out of the gondola. Sadie screamed, but Oliver held his nerve. At first, the twister kept him out of reach of the docking ring, but he remained patient, and eventually, he was able to wrap his leg around the rope that was keeping the Rebel in dangerously close proximity to the tree. At times, the rope went slack, and sometimes, the wind snapped it taut. The combination of rain and the strength of the wind tightening the knot had made it too difficult to untie it, so Oliver proceeded to saw through the rope with his knife. He had almost sliced through it when an object caught up in the storm hit him from behind, and in surprise, Oliver dropped the knife. At first, Oliver was annoyed because he hadn't quite completed the job, but a few seconds later, the last strands of the rope snapped and the Rebel was free of the tree. Then it dawned on Oliver that he was still in grave danger because he was outside the gondola, and not only was there a tree spinning uncontrollably in close pursuit of them, but a sharp knife had joined it. He didn't want to come in contact with either!

'Up! Up!' he yelled. The wind carried away Oliver's voice, but it didn't matter because Jake had been watching carefully and started the motor on the winch that would bring his friend back to the safety of the gondola. Once inside, Oliver called to Charlotte, 'Take us up higher - up into the clouds and away from that damned tree and my knife!' Then, utterly exhausted, he collapsed onto the deck to a round of applause from the crew.

It wasn't until two hours later that Charlotte felt she was fully in control of the airship, and the tornado had finally blown on to wreak havoc elsewhere.

'Let me take over,' said Oliver, untying the rope that bound Charlotte and Sadie to the helm. 'You need some rest.' The women nodded in agreement, and they both settled down to sleep. Sadie, having held on to Charlotte through such a dangerous fight with Mother Nature, was not inclined to let go now.

'Blimey!' said Billy, sitting on the deck behind a chair. The crew realised that it had been quite a long time since they had heard him speak. 'That was a bloomin strange old snooze. I started off 'aving a kip on that chair over there, and I've woken up over here on the flamin' floor. I've had a bleedin' crazy old dream! I fort I was on a bloomin' merry-go-round. Would you Adam an' Eve it!'

'Where are we, Jake? Have you any idea?' asked Charlotte.

'I'm sorry, but we've been blown so far off course that the only thing I can safely say is that we are still in America,' replied Jake. 'I'm afraid our maps lack the detail we need to identify our position. After all, this is the wild, wild west; much of it is uncharted territory.'

'But I don't even know whether I should fly North, South, East or West,' moaned Charlotte.

'There's a railway line down there,' observed Jake, 'Why don't you follow it?'

'Good idea,' said Oliver, 'Sooner or later, we are bound to come across some kind of settlement, and we can go down and ask them where we are.'

Twenty minutes later, Billy called out:

'I seen summat! Yer should think yourself bloomin' lucky 'cause I got such good bleedin' minces!'

'What the heck are you talking about, Billy?' asked Sadie.

'Minces - mince pies - eyes! There's an 'ouse over there.'

'So there is,' confirmed Jake. 'It looks like a farmhouse. Or should I say a ranch? Let's go and introduce ourselves.'

Usually, Joshua liked to shimmy down the rope to dock the airship, but everyone was concerned that his bullet wound might open up if he was too energetic, so this time Jake was the first to reach the ground. He tied the rope to what would once have been the corral It was redundant now there were no horses and the gate to the enclosure swung open, creaking on its rusty hinges. Once the airship was secure, Oliver unfurled the rope ladder, and the rest of the crew descended.

'I'll tell yer what,' said Billy, 'It's nice to be back on bleedin' terry firma again! Not sure what Terry finks about bein' trampled on, but I'm certainly enjoyin' it. Who was he, anyway?'

There was no time for a reply because the crew heard

the front door to the ranch open and saw a woman standing in the doorway, aiming a double-barreled shotgun at them.

'What are you doing on my property? Who are you? Are you Carter's men?'

'Allow me to introduce ourselves,' said Oliver, 'My name is Oliver Moon, and collectively we are known as the Rebel Runaways. I can tell you everyone's name in due course, but to answer your questions - no, we are not Carter's men. In fact, I've no idea who he is, and as you can see, we aren't all men. We have simply dropped by to ask directions, after which we will bother you no more.'

'What d'ya mean you don't know Carter? Everyone knows that thievin', bullyin' son of a bitch round here.'

'Ah! We are not from these parts, Madam. We are lost in a strange land,' replied Oliver.

'How did you get here anyway? I always keep one eye on who's coming down the trail.'

'We came from a different direction,' said Oliver, pointing up at the Rebel.

'Well I'll be...! I ain't seen nothing like that before. How does it stay up there?

'Madam, if you would be so kind as to lower your gun, I would be happy to answer all your questions,'

'I'm sorry, I'm forgetting my manners. My name's Rosa May. Would you folks like a cup of coffee?'

No sooner had the Rebel Runaways seated themselves around the kitchen table than Rosa stood up and reached for her gun.

'Now, they look like Carter's men coming down the track,' she said.

'Who is this Carter chap?' asked Oliver, 'He seems extremely unpopular in your household. Persona non grata,

I would even venture to say.'

'I fort she said 'is name was Carter not Grata!' piped up Billy.

'It means he's someone who isn't welcome,' explained Charlotte.

'He most definitely isn't welcome here,' said Rosa, 'He's the biggest landowner in these parts, and he's been trying to force us off our land for years. And talk of the devil, those are his men, now.'

Rosa opened the door and stood calmly, her rifle at her shoulder. The crew rushed to the window to see three men approach the ranch, all looking in amazement at the Rebel, gently swaying in the wind.

'What do you want?' shouted Rosa.

'Well, would you look at that?' said the nearest man, ignoring her question, 'What you got there, Rosa?'

'That's none of your business. I know you, Jed. The three of you wouldn't walk all the way here just for the exercise. What do you want?'

'We're mighty thirsty, Rosa,' said Jed.

'A cup of coffee to wash away the trail dust would be appreciated, Rosa,' added one of his companions.

'It's Mrs May to you, Silas,' she snapped, 'You can help yourself to water from the well.'

'Frank Carter asked us to have a word with you. He was wonderin' if you had reconsidered his offer,' said a third man.

'He's only got your best interests at heart. Isn't that right Pete? He knows your husband is driving cattle to Cedar Creek, and Frank's worried about what you would do if he had some kind of accident,' said Jed. 'Accidents easily happen.'

'Well, you've wasted your time - you can fill up your

water bottles, and then you can get off my property.'

'There's no need for that tone of voice, Rosa, and you don't need that gun. Just one friendly cup of coffee and...' Jed's voice trailed off as Oliver opened the door fully and stood behind Rosa, flanked by the imposing figure of Joshua.

'I think Mrs May has said all she needs to say on the subject,' said Oliver.

'Jake unlatched the window. 'Help yourself to water,' he called, 'Enjoy your walk back.'

Jed looked at Jake and could make out more figures behind him. He scowled as he could see that he and his two companions were outnumbered.

'Frank said you should think about it. It's a fair offer, all things considered. You never know what might happen,' said Jed. Then the three men turned and headed towards the well.

Rosa closed the door and placed the kettle on the stove.

'I'm sorry this coffee's a long time coming,' she said, 'I was expecting them boys to show up. I knew word would get out that my husband, Johnny, would be away for a few days, and now I'm worried about Johnny's safety.'

'May I call you Rosa?' asked Oliver. Rosa nodded, 'Then perhaps, Rosa, you will allow the Rebel Runaways to help!'

CHAPTER ELEVEN

'We've seen city life in New York, but how has it been here in the country since the horses all died?' asked Charlotte.

'Everything changed,' replied Rosa, 'Including the colour of my hair. Look, do you see all this grey? That wasn't there before the horse flu came. I'm only forty, but I feel and look twenty years older. We are trying to adapt, but it's hard for the body and the mind. We took it for granted that horses would always be around. I've been riding since I was three and feel like I've lost part of my family.'

'It must be tough for you,' commiserated Sadie.

'It's hit the menfolk even harder,' Rosa continued, 'The towns are full of cowboys who spend what little money they have on liquor. Riding a horse was something that signified being a man, and now that's been stolen from them, they don't know how to prove themselves other than by drinking and fighting. There are some mean and crazy folk out there.'

'It's a big, big country if you have to walk everywhere,' said Oliver.

'That's true. This is cattle country, and we breed Devons here. Mostly, they can look after themselves; it's good grazing land and they roam free. We're a small ranch, but we still have a lot of land, so it takes a lot of walking to round them up. In the old days, my husband, Johnny and our son, Ben, could manage the ranch with just a few hired hands. Then, when it was time to take the cattle to market, we'd take on a team of around ten boys to drive them cross-country to Cedar Creek.'

'What happened at Cedar Creek?' asked Sadie.

'The cattle were sold and then sent North by railroad. It was a hard enough journey when we had horses, so you can imagine what it's like on foot! What makes it worse is that after the horses died, some of our men quit. They were accustomed to riding - they weren't going to walk! Most of the others were poached by Carter because he could afford to pay higher wages. Now there's just Johnny and a few old-timers left to get the cattle to market.'

'Is that why you don't like Carter, for stealing your men?' asked Joshua.

'It sure don't help. It's more than that, though. When my grandfather built this ranch, land was cheap - we own as far as you can see in all directions. Everything was fine and dandy until Carter came to these parts. He bought the ranches from a couple of good old boys on either side of us. So now we are sandwiched between parcels of Carter's land, and he wants to buy ours to make one big spread. We won't sell, though. I saw what happened to Seb MacMurdy from the ranch next door. The money didn't do him any good - he just drank himself to death in the Cedar Creek saloons.'

'We noticed the railroad came through here,' commented Jake, 'It's a pity you can't transport the cattle by train from here.'

'You noticed that, did you?' laughed Rosa, 'I suppose you get a good view from up there. Apart from this ranch being in our family for three generations, four when Ben takes over, that's another reason why we won't sell. You see, the railroad cuts diagonally across our land - it doesn't cross Carter's land. When the railroad first came, my father resisted it; he didn't like change, but now, especially since the horse flu, Johnny thinks it could be our saving.'

'It would certainly save a lot of bleedin' walkin',' laughed Billy.

'More than that; Johnny has dreams,' said Rosa. 'Did you notice the river that crosses our land?' Jake and Charlotte nodded, 'And to the North, there is a forest. Johnny spends his time making maps. He's certain that this would be a perfect place to build a new town. Timber, water and a railroad. A perfect combination. It might be that Carter is also thinking along similar lines.'

'Speaking of your husband, Rosa, I think it's time we set off to find him,' said Oliver, 'Joshua is going to stay with you in case Carter's men return. Are you all set with your gadgets, Jake!'

'Nearly. I can sort out the finishing touches when we are in the air,' replied Jake.

'Then let's go and wrangle some cows,' yelled Oliver.

'Is that 'ow yer cook 'em?' asked Billy, 'I don't fink I got a fryin' pan big enough!'

'Hooray!' cried Charlotte, 'I see them.'

'Good,' said Jake, 'If we were flying through grey English skies, we could go up above the clouds so as not to scare the cows and cause a stampede. But unfortunately there's nothing up here but clear blue sky, so I'll chart a course to fly around them, and then you can drop us off further along the trail.

'I've got the letter of introduction from Rosa here,' said Oliver, patting his pocket. 'We don't want Johnny and his men thinking we're rustlers.'

Thirty minutes later, Oliver, Jake, Billy and Sadie were waiting patiently for Johnny and the herd to arrive. Charlotte had circled the Rebel back to the rear of the cattle drive, where she could follow unobserved.

Sadie was grinning from ear to ear. Jake had, at last, finished constructing a scooter for her - now they each had one.

'Ee! I can't wait to try it out!'

Jake had also made one for Billy, but Billy was more reticent about showing his appreciation.

'Don't look so worried, Billy,' said Jake, 'Yours has a trailer fitted, so it makes the mono-scoot very stable. It will be hard to fall off.'

'If it's bloomin' well possible to fall off, don't worry, I flamin' well will.'

'Just don't try to go too fast,' advised Jake, 'I've geared the clockwork motor to make it efficient for pulling heavy loads. You only need to activate the steam boost canister when climbing a steep hill. Think of all the food and cooking utensils you can transport!' Billy nodded glumly, still apprehensive about using it. 'But yours, Madam,' said Jake to Sadie, 'Has been built for speed. Mind you, you should avoid using the steam boost except in an emergency. I have a few spare canisters, but there will be nowhere to replenish the compressed steam out here in the country.'

'Does it fire darts like I wanted it to?' asked Sadie.

'Yes, there's a button underneath that red safety cap, but please, try to avoid killing people unless you really have to. Go on. Have a quick practice before the drovers get here. Practise riding, I mean, not killing people!'

'Hell! That's the darnedest thing I ever seen!' chuckled Rooster, watching Sadie slowly circle around them on her mono-scoot as they sat around the campfire finishing their beans. Rooster was the cook, and he'd earned that nickname because of his delight in tossing any tough old bird wandering too far from the roost into the stew.

'I appreciate you being with us on the drive. We ain't never had women along with us before, but we need all the help we can get!' commented Johnny.

'Sadie isn't like other women,' chuckled Oliver. 'Woe betide any man that upsets her.'

'But maybe,' continued Rooster, standing and turning on the spot as he watched Sadie, 'Maybe that takes the biscuit.' Rooster pointed towards the airship in the distance.

'So it looks like we have a plan,' said Oliver. 'Jake and Sadie can circle the herd and round up any strays.'

'Gently, mind!' warned Johnny. 'If they get spooked, we might lose them in a stampede.' Oliver and Jake nodded.

'I'll walk with you men; just tell me what to do, and Billy can help Rooster pull the chuck wagon,' said Oliver,

'It's gonna be a helluva lot easier with two of us,' said Rooster.

'Not only that, it won't be so bloomin' heavy because we can offload a lot of the supplies into the Rebel, and Charlotte can bring 'em,' added Billy, 'Then I can collect them in my scooty-truck. Bloomin' thing!' He eyed it with distrust; true to his word, he had fallen off it at the first attempt, even though he had only been travelling at a snail's pace.

'Do you reckon I could ride it?' asked Rooster.

'Be my guest, mate, be my bleedin' guest!'

The next few days settled into a pattern which mainly consisted of following behind the cattle, coaxing them to go in the right direction, and eating a lot of dust kicked up by their hooves. This was followed by a supper of beans swilled down with bitter coffee as the men sat around the campfire spinning yarns and tall tales late into the night. By then, Sadie was always back on the airship for the night.

'I'm sure I could tether the Rebel to a tree and come and join you,' suggested Charlotte.

'Perhaps you should come and say hello sometime, but to be perfectly honest, I would much rather be here with you than down there. You know what men are like when they get together. So much hot air and, on account of the beans, it's coming from both ends! Jake's trying to figure out how to harness those powerful forces of nature to propel the rebel!'

Once their laughter had subsided, Charlotte turned to more practical matters.

'Rosa was worried that Carter might spring a nasty

surprise, so I think we ought to be vigilant. I'm going to fly ahead occasionally and check if anyone is waiting to ambush you.'

'Good idea,' said Sadie.

'There's something else too,' said Charlotte, gesturing to the sacks that Billy had offloaded from the chuck wagon. 'I don't think there's enough food. We have some of our own, but we were planning to have replenished our supplies by now, and the cowboys weren't expecting four extra mouths to feed. I think I should take Billy to find the nearest town and stock up. You and Jake are more useful for rounding up cattle on your scooty-things, and I daren't take Oliver. One good thing about this trip is that the cowboys haven't got anything stronger than coffee with them. Once Oliver rolls into a town, it will be hard getting him out of the first saloon he sees.'

'True,' agreed Sadie. 'He'll have a thirst on. I'll tell you what I need, though. Not a drink, but a bath. I reckon I must look a sight.'

'You are rather dusty!' laughed Charlotte. 'As the men aren't around, now would be an ideal time. We've plenty of water. I'll help you.'

'I'd like that, I really would,' whispered Sadie.

Joshua winced as he stooped to pick up the logs he had been splitting.

'Are you sure you are fit enough to do that?' asked Rosa.

'I'm healing just fine,' replied Joshua, 'I just moved too fast, that's all.'

'Let me help you anyway,' said Rosa, piling logs into a

basket and carrying them to the log store. 'Then I'll go and fix us some breakfast.'

'Do you know,' said Joshua a little while later, smacking his lips, 'Since I met Oliver and the other Rebel Runaways, I've been eating some pretty fancy foods, but I had forgotten just how good biscuits and gravy taste. You can't get them in England.'

'My son, Ben, always used to say, "You can't beat Momma's cooking," and who am I to disagree with him?' laughed Rosa.

'Let's hope he approves of Billy's cooking,' replied Joshua, joining in with the laughter, 'The boy's improving, though - you should have tasted his first attempts at rock cakes. I tell you, they were closer to rocks than cakes.'

'Oh! Ben's not on the cattle trail with my husband.'

'I'm sorry, I just assumed he was. He's... he's still alive is he? Has my big mouth gone and said the wrong thing?' Rosa went quiet and all the good humour drained from her face.

'Pray God he's still alive. I haven't heard from him for weeks. Ben went off to fight. We didn't want him to go, but we are proud of him all the same. My Ben's joined the army. He said, "Momma, I know you need me to help Pa on the ranch, but if me and the boys don't go to war, then who's gonna stop them damn Yankees from taking over our farm or burning us out?" And I know he was right, but that doesn't stop me worrying about him. I pray every day that he comes home alive.' The kitchen fell silent for a moment before Joshua spoke again.

'So, he's joined the Confederate Army?'

'Of course, he has. Who else is going to protect folk like me?' In the long pause that followed, Rosa studied Joshua's face. 'I know what you are thinking,' she said, breaking the silence, 'You are thinking that we are all fighting to keep slavery. Well, you are wrong. Do you see any slaves around here? As far back as you can go in both Johnny's and my history, no one has ever owned a slave. Nor wanted to. We work hard, and we stick together as a family. Our land is our land, and we will fight anyone who tries to take it. Do you know what would happen if the Yankees marched in here? They would steal our cattle. They might say "requisition", but I say steal. They would feed our cattle to their army or else send them up North and sell them to pampered city folk to pay for guns and bullets to kill our children. Of course, he's a Confederate!' Rosa reached out and placed her hand on Joshua's. 'You may be black, son, and I may be white, but we are all God's children. Life is not so simple as being black or white. It's a whole lot more complicated than that. Now, are you going to finish those biscuits and gravy or not?'

Joshua looked down at his plate, popped a forkful in his mouth and smiled.

'I sure am. I don't suppose you got any more?'

DAVE JOHNSON

CHAPTER TWELVE

Children ran from one house to another, spreading the news, and soon, almost everyone in the small town of Dry Gulch was out on the streets, looking up, open-mouthed in amazement.

'Cor blimey, I don't mind tellin' ya, I'm a bit bloomin' nervous,' said Billy to Charlotte, waving to the crowds below. 'I 'ope no one's goin' to be taking bleedin' pot-shots at me.'

'I can't see why anyone would feel threatened by you,' replied Charlotte. 'If they were worried about our arrival, surely they would have been shooting at us already.'

'Well, 'ere goes, wish me luck,' said Billy as he strapped himself into the winch, 'Don't wind her up in case we 'ave to bleedin' scarper!'

In the event, Billy need not have worried. When the diminutive East-End boy, dressed in his rainbow finest, landed on the dusty main street, children thronged around him and men, initially suspicious, shook their heads, smiled and holstered their pistols.

'Ere! I ain't done nuffing!' called Billy, 'It's Charlotte wot's flying the airship. I've just come to do a spot of bloomin' shopping.' It didn't stop the children dancing excitedly around him. Some even reached out to touch him, checking that he was real. They escorted him up and down the town, which was little more than a single street, proudly pointing out the Sherrif's office, the undertakers and the saloon. Finally, they led him into the general store and gazed in wonder at the exotic visitor as he made his purchases.

'Much obliged to you,' said the storekeeper, slipping Billy's money into a drawer. A group of children lined the back of the store to watch the visitor from the skies. More children were outside, their necks craned, looking up at the Rebel hovering above them and waving whenever Charlotte left the controls and appeared in the doorway to wave back.

'Do you want to give me a hand to carry all these provisions out into the street?' Billy asked the children. They darted forward, tripping over themselves in their eagerness. 'Then, when Charlotte lowers a basket, you can load it up.'

'Well, I never,' chuckled the storekeeper, 'I ain't never seen such a commotion in this little town before. The whole place is a buzzin'!'

'I couldn't help noticing that there was one fella who couldn't care less,' replied Billy. 'Lying on the bleedin' street, he was. Didn't even turn his bloomin' head! I said hello an' all.'

'Ah, that'll be old Pete. He'll be drunk, if someone has fetched him a bottle of whisky, or else he's asleep. He doesn't move from that spot on account of only having one foot. He had two feet when he rode into town from Sourwater, but he caught some disease. The doctor said it was called Dying Beeties, or some such. Anyroad, then the horse flu came, and he was in no fit state to walk out of here, so here he stays. Actually, he started off outside my store, but we had to move him further down the street because he smells so bad.'

'That's a bleedin' sad story,' said Billy, shaking his head.

'Some of the womenfolk bring him food now and then; he's got some money behind the bar at the saloon to pay for his whisky, and I've got his funeral money in a jar up on that there shelf.'

'Pwoar!' said Billy under his breath, 'I know what the storekeeper meant about the smell. He's like a human latrine.' Billy crouched down and gently prodded the recumbent man on the arm. 'Pete, Pete. My name's Billy. Is there anything you need?' Pete opened his eyes and studied Billy for a moment.

'Boy,' he replied in a hoarse whisper. 'I need to get outta this town before it kills me.'

'Well, if ya don't mind me sayin', I fink this town 'as got the upper hand.' Pete laughed. 'Wait here a moment,' said Billy, springing to his feet. 'I just got to 'ave a natter wiv Charlotte.'

'I ain't going anywhere, son.'

Charlotte had already stowed away most of the provisions.

'Don't go yet,' said Billy, dragging a sack of beans across the floor. 'I've got some stuff to talk about. First of all, you know how you and Sadie used up nearly all the bleedin' water 'aving a bloomin' bath?' Charlotte blushed. 'Well,' continued Billy, 'As you can imagine, in a town called Dry Gulch, there 'ain't a river 'ere, but I asked where there is one, and it ain't far. Now, as it 'appens, I've met someone who could do wiv a bath. Boy, could he do with a bath, so can we give him a ride? There's a good chance he might poison all the fish in the river, but that ain't our concern.'

For the second time that day, pretty much the whole town assembled on the street as Smelly Pete was hoisted up into the sky.

'Here you are, son,' said the storekeeper, handing over a jar to Billy. 'That's his funeral fund. I've topped it up with the money he left behind the bar in the saloon. Frankly, my boy, as well as helping Pete, you are doing the whole town a favour because we were embarrassed that we couldn't do more to help him. And you are doing me a personal favour because when we were downwind of him, the smell used to put customers off coming into the store.'

'I'm not sure Charlotte will let him aboard the bloomin' airship,' laughed Billy. 'I've opened all the bleedin' windows, but we might have to dangle 'im outside until we get to the river.'

'Take this, son, you'll need it!' Billy grinned as the storekeeper dropped a large bar of soap into his outstretched hand.

An hour later, Charlotte was back at the helm on a course that would lead them back to find the cattle drive.

'We can shut the bleedin' windows now,' chirped Billy, looking over to Pete, lying exhausted from the day's exertions. 'It's a good fit, that suit of Jake's. One fing you can be certain of, there was no bleedin' way that Charlotte was goin' to let your own clothes on board again. I left them on the river bank, but they've probably run off on their own. They woz rank! The good news is that in a couple of days' time, we won't be far from Sourwater, so we can take you back to your own gaff.'

'Gaff?' queried Pete.

'Your home, mate. Anyway, as soon as we catch up with the others, we can stop, and I'll climb down, make a fire, and brew a nice pot of rosy lee.'

'Rosy lee?'

'Rosy Lee - tea.'

'Ah! 'Why didn't you say so? I knew a woman called Rosa once. When I still lived on the ranch.'

'Now that we've got you all spruced up, Pete, I expect you'll be meeting lots of women.' laughed Billy. The old man shook his head at the absurdity of the idea.

'There they are!' shouted Charlotte. 'I can see the herd up ahead!'

If Billy had thought Pete looked smart after his bath, it was nothing compared with how he looked once Sadie had finished with him.

'Ee lad, You look grand!' she said, holding up a mirror for him to admire his newly trimmed hair and beard. Pete chuckled, both at the sight of himself in the glass and at being called a lad by Sadie when he was probably three times her age. He laughed even louder when Billy reappeared.

'Cor Blimey, who's stolen Santa? I was relying on us havin' 'im aboard to get some presents for once.' Billy was Pete's favourite, and they spent a fair bit of time together nattering because Billy no longer had to help Rooster pull the chuck wagon. Jake had repaired the harness they had used to scoop up the submersible, and now, with a few alterations, they were using it to pick up the whole wagon, fly ahead and set it down on the trail where Billy would boil up the beans and wait for the cowboys to catch up. Nothing would induce Rooster to travel in the airship; he preferred to walk with the others, and they were grateful for an extra hand to coax the cattle to travel in the right direction.

'So why did you go to Dry Gulch in the first place?' asked Billy, 'It ain't exactly a place for sightseeing.'

'I was just wandering through,' replied Pete. 'I have a room over in Sourwater, but I spent a good bit of the last thirty years on the move. I guess I just felt restless.'

'So, 'ow did you pay your way? Were all the pretty women showering you wiv gifts?'

'I was lucky. I hit a good seam prospecting for gold so I had plenty of cash for a while but it's beginning to run out. There's a few dollars left in the bank in Sourwater. Maybe there's enough left to see me out.' Billy contemplated the jar of funeral money that he was keeping safe for Pete and a sadness descended on him.

'Aven't you got any family?'

'I had a wife and a baby son, but I lost them both to smallpox. I like to think my boy would have grown up like you, son.'

'Bleedin' 'ell. I wouldn't wish that on anyone!'

'I've got a brother, but I don't see him no more. We had a big argument after Pa died, and I walked away from the ranch. I guess I've been travelling ever since.'

'Now the 'orses' ave all bleedin' well died, and you can't go walking coz you ain't got the right number of feet, you'll 'ave to try hoppin'! But I know what you mean about family; my Mum was in the flamin' Nick last I 'eard, an' me Dad's been sent to the uvver end of the world to bloomin' 'Stralia. My two bruvvers and my sister ain't bovvered about me, so the Rebel Runaways are my family.'

'I think my hoppin' days are over, Billy. Maybe I should have buried the hatchet with my brother, but there's too much water under the bridge now.'

Once again, Billy's arrival was creating a stir; this time in Sourwater. Charlotte had stopped a little way out of town and lowered Pete, Billy and the mono-scoot Billy used to transport food, which he had christened the Chucky-Scoot. Then, after strapping Pete to the trailer they proceeded to Pete's hotel room.

'I told you yer shouldn't 'ave shaved off that long beard of yours, Pete. You would definitely 'ave looked like Santa arrivin' on his sleigh! On the other 'and, they might call me bloomin' Rudolph, so p'raps it's just as well you did.' It could truly have been Santa arriving, judging by the reaction from Sourwater's children. They skipped and sang as they accompanied Billy and Pete into town. Eventually, Pete pointed out his hotel, and with Billy on one side and the help of a crutch that Jake had made, Pete found the way to his room. Billy opened the shutters and Pete flopped onto the bed with a contented sigh.

'I tell you, boy, I'm all done in. That's me finished, I reckon.'

'Coz we've flown ahead of the herd to get here, Charlotte says I can come back again tomorrow to see you,' said Billy. 'The blitherin' cows won't 'ave walked much furver.'

'You could do one last thing for me before you go,' said Pete, 'Go into the saloon and ask for a feller called Dan White. He's bound to be there. He always wears black, and he's got long silver hair and a droopy moustache. Ask him to come and see me tonight. Tell him to wake me if I'm asleep.'

'Sure fing, Hopalong!' replied Billy cheerfully. 'And then there's a few dozen children wants a ride on me Santa sleigh.'

'You can't stay long,' warned Charlotte, 'I'll have to fly at top speed to catch up with the herd.'

'Nah! Don't you worry. I just wanna say me goodbyes,' replied Billy.

'I'll just circle slowly around the town. There aren't any trees to tie the Rebel up to here.'

Billy breezed into the hotel. A man mopping the floor looked up and recognised Billy from the day before.

'Excuse me...' he began, but Billy was already leaping up the stairs.

'S'alright, I knows me way!' called Billy, as he disappeared round a corner. He rapped on Pete's door and went straight in. 'Hey, Hopalong,' he called, then his voice trailed off. The room was dark, but he could see that it was empty. As he opened the shutters, Billy heard a knock at the door, and the man from downstairs entered.

'I was a tryin' to tell you. Pete ain't here no more. He died last night, and the undertaker has fetched him. They gonna be burying him this morning because Pete didn't have no family, well, none we knows about. He left you this note which says for you to find Dan White.'

'What did he go and do that for?' cried Billy, as he stumbled out of the room, blinded by tears.

An hour later, Charlotte was desperately worried. Billy should have been back by now, but there was no sign of him. She felt helpless; it seemed too risky to take the airship into town, find somewhere to tie her up, and then leave the Rebel to look for Billy. What if she ended up losing the airship in the process, or some drunken gunslinger used it for target practice? Charlotte had no choice; she needed help - she had to find the rest of the Rebel Runaways.

It was another three hours before the airship returned. Oliver, Jake and Sadie climbed down the rope ladder and strode resolutely into town. Sadie was wearing her Glove and Jake was similarly armed with his dart-firing hand. Some children guessed why they had come and ran to offer advice.

'This way,' said one, and the Rebels followed the sombre little group of children to the saloon. It took a while for their eyes to get accustomed to the gloom, and then they noticed Billy slumped over a table with an empty whisky bottle lying on its side in front of him. Nearby stood a tall man dressed in black with long silver hair.

'Billy!' gasped Sadie, and marched over to Billy's companion. 'How dare you!' she yelled and raised her arm to fire the Glove. Jake had anticipated her reaction and raced forward to stop her,

'Hear him out,' he commanded.

'It ain't what you think. My name's Dan White, and I'm the notary around these parts.' Seeing Sadie's puzzled expression, he added, 'That means I authenticate documents, which makes 'em legal. I use this place as my office because people know where to find me here. It's handy, too, because of the number of times I've had to witness documents for people handing over the deeds for the property they'd lost in a card game! Anyway, this boy's friend, Pete MacMurdy, asked me to come and see him yesterday because he wanted to write a will. Which I duly did, and then a few hours later, he upped and died. We buried him two hours ago. The boy's taken it very badly.'

'Thank you for your help, kind Sir,' replied Oliver, fighting hard to resist the urge to buy them both a drink. 'We can help him back to our airship.'

'Not so fast,' replied Dan White, 'I was waiting for the boy to sober up. Pete has left him something in his will. I was worried he might lose it if I gave it to him while he was drunk.' Dan handed Oliver an envelope and went on to explain: 'It's the deeds to a strip of land that was left to Pete by his Pa. It's the reason why he fell out with his brother, who isn't alive any more. When I say a strip, I mean it's miles long, but it's only a foot wide. You can step over it. His brother had the right of way over it, but no one else! You will have to take this document to Cedar Creek to get it ratified.'

'That's where we are heading anyway,' said Sadie, having slipped her Glove back in her bag.'

'MacMurdy. Where have I heard that name before?' pondered Jake.

CHAPTER THIRTEEN

My dearest Jessy,

Even if I knew where I was going next, I wouldn't be able to tell you because the news might get back to the Confederacy, and they would be waiting for me. Then again, I suppose by the time you get this, I'll be somewhere else, so maybe I should tell you because then they would be waiting in the wrong place.

If you were wondering why my writing has gotten a lot better, it's because I have someone new helping me. The other feller got himself killed. My new friend is called Isaac; he seems to have a survival instinct and he's got my back. We look out for each other. I'm sorry for him because he ain't got any kin, and that makes me feel extra lucky because I got you for my sweetheart, and I'm hoping somewhere I've still got a sister.

Im riting this last bit on my own. I jest want to put that I love you, and I allus will.

Kisses,

Luke.

'Put yourself in Frank Carter's place, said Oliver. 'If you were planning mischief, where would you do it? I don't know the terrain between here and Cedar Creek.' Johnny threw another log on the fire, took a sip of coffee, and nodded.

'I've been thinking about this. I didn't want to worry you, so I ain't said anything yet.'

'Me? Worry? Nothing worries me,' replied Oliver. Jake laughed, knowing it to be true. Drunk or sober, Oliver took everything in his stride.

'They ain't coming from behind. It would take too much effort to catch us up, and as we are on the plains we would see them coming. It makes more sense to get ahead of us and sit and wait. In three days' time, we should reach a mountain range, and we have to travel through Dead Man's Gulch. It's a narrow pass, and if the cattle stampeded while we were travellin' through, we would all be goners. Yep, that's where I would choose.'

'The cows look better from up here than down there,' said Sadie, gazing through the window at the herd in the distance. 'It were a novelty at first, especially riding me scooty-bob, but now it's just plain borin'. It's not so bad when one of 'em wanders off and I have to go and round it up, but to tell you the truth, sometimes I feel like wandering off meself!'

'At least you and Jake are on the edge of the herd,' commented Billy, 'And I'm usually up ahead , with the chuck wagon. Think wot it's like for poor old Rooster at the back of the cows. Chewin' flamin' dust.'

'Sometimes I think that would be better than 'aving to chew flamin' beans every day,' moaned Sadie.

'I notice you ain't walkin' at the back no more, Oliver,' laughed Billy.

'Well, a brave general always leads from the front,' chuckled Oliver. 'Has your hangover gone now, Billy?'

'Yes, it took its bleedin' time.'

'And have you come to terms with old Pete passing?' asked Charlotte.

'S'pose.'

'Think of it this way - befriending Pete and cleaning him up allowed him to die with dignity. He was an old man who wasn't well, so he felt it was time to go.' Billy nodded but turned to face the window and pretended to be interested in the view so the others wouldn't see that his eyes were growing moist.

'Time I got a little shuteye. Wake me when we get close to Dead Man's Gulch,' said Oliver, stretching out and yawning.

'Remember, this is just a reconnaissance mission,' said Oliver, scanning the gap in the mountain range through a telescope, 'So, we shan't get nearer than we need to. We won't take any chances and will keep the element of surprise for when we return. I can see the pass ahead, so take her five degrees to starboard, Charlotte, and we will skirt right around them and come in from the other direction. They probably won't be looking that way, and in any case, if we keep low, their view will be impeded by the mountain.'

A little while later, they glided above one flank of the gorge.

'From this angle, that big boulder on the top looks like a giant pussy cat,' laughed Sadie.

'I have an idea,' cried Jake. 'Set me down here and then stay out of sight. I'll creep up and look over the top.'

'Be careful,' warned Oliver. 'I can see a lot of loose shingle. It will be slippy underfoot.'

Jake took just a few minutes to peer around the boulder on top of the mountain, then he slid back the way he had come and signalled for the Rebel to drop the rope ladder.

'Well? Did ya get a good butcher's?' asked Billy excitedly. Jake had grown accustomed to Billy's Cockney rhyming slang.

'Yes, Billy, I saw at least three men. You wouldn't spot them from the bottom of the gorge as they are tucked in behind rocks. They have rifles trained down on the pass. It would only take a few shots ricocheting around the mountain sides to send the cattle into a mad stampede. But don't worry, I have a plan; we can return to the drovers now.'

'We should get back in time to get a bowl of beans,' chirped Billy. Sadie groaned at the thought.

'I'm not sure how many more days I can put up with being a cowgirl,' complained Sadie. 'I'm on my feet all day; it's dusty, and the only thing I've got to keep me company are cows. And more cows. It's been alright for you, Jake - you've been up here in the Rebel for the last two days fiddling wi' your cogs and springs an' whatnot.'

'Depending on how today goes, the end will be in sight soon. The herd will take half a day to reach Dead Man's Gulch, and then, if the team can get through the pass, we will reach Cedar Creek after another two days,' said Oliver. 'I must say, Jake, I'm intrigued to know what you have been making. I can see you have cannibalised the Rebel.'

'I'm sorry about that; I needed a few metal struts, and obviously, I couldn't buy them in this...this wilderness,' replied Jake.

'Is it some kind of catapult?' asked Charlotte.

'You can wait and see. If it doesn't work, we will have to resort to plan B.'

'What is plan B?' asked Sadie.

'We will lower Oliver onto the mountain, and he can fight them all,' laughed Jake.

'I really can't see why that isn't Plan A,' said Oliver indignantly.

'Charlotte,' instructed Jake, 'Follow the same course as before, please. Drop me off near that boulder, and then stay out of sight.

On a ridge overlooking the pass, three extremely bored men were crouching behind rocks with a good view of the route that the cattle drive would have to take.

'I reckon I can see dust in the distance, Boss. They'll be here before the day is out.'

'If I gets a good sight, do you want me to shoot 'em,

boss?'

'I told you, Jed, you idiot, no!' hissed Carter. 'It's got to look like the cattle just got spooked and stampeded. If Johnny May and his men get crushed to death in the confusion, then so be it. But it will be no good if they get found with bullet in 'em.'

'Oh yeah, Boss. I forgot.'

'If the cattle run off, they will have lost all their investment, and I can buy the farm at a knockdown price. If Johnny is killed, the result will be the same.'

'Looks like you are gonna win either way,' cackled the third man.

'I always win, Eli,' replied Carter smugly.

High above them and well out of earshot, Jake dug away at the loose earth beneath the boulder that the crew had christened the 'Pussycat'. Then he forced the contraption he had built into the channel beneath the rock and wound up the clockwork motor. Jake waved at the Rebel, hovering nearby, then returned to his machine.

'What shall I call you?' he wondered, 'I know! Larry the Lever! Go on, Larry. Do your worst!' Jake pressed a button and the device slowly began to work. Cogs whirred, engaging other cogs, pressing the device against the rock. Rods shot out sideways to steady the machine and prevent it from tipping over as it exerted more and more pressure. Jake slithered down the mountain a short distance; there was no more he could do other than call encouragement.

'Come on Larry, nice and steady does it.' Jake was confident that his calculations were correct and that the gearing would withstand the weight of the heavy boulder. Little by little, Larry the Lever began to open out into a wedge shape, pushing against the boulder, when suddenly the rock began to move and then slip and slide down the other side of the mountain. Jake scrambled back up to the peak and saw the 'Pussycat' gathering speed and crashing into other rocks, which joined it as it hurtled down the slope. Jake grabbed Larry the Lever and waved for Charlotte to bring the Rebel. He wanted a better view.

'What's that noise?' shouted Eli. Jed had heard that sound before; he didn't need to look and he scrambled around the rock that he had been hiding behind. Eli saw him and followed suit. Carter, however, was more used to giving orders than taking them and, instead of moving, he turned to look at the source of the roaring as it reached a terrifying crescendo. He only paused for a moment, but it was a moment too long, and before he could move, a shower of rocks and boulders rained down on him, pinning him to the ground.

Above them, with Jake by their side, Billy and Oliver trained their telescopes on the avalanche's path.

'Cor blimey, that sure is one bleedin' angry pussycat!' exclaimed Billy.

'It's difficult to see what's happening down there with all the dust,' murmured Oliver, 'No, wait. I can see two men who appear to be trying to remove a pile of rocks. I presume someone is underneath them. We'll wait a while and observe. Let's see if they resume their positions guarding the pass.'

'Boss! Are you alright?' cried Jed, scrabbling at the rocks.

'Aagh! Get me out of here!' roared Carter. Twenty minutes later, Jed and Eli looked down with concern at their employer, who lay groaning on the ground.

'I reckon that arm is broken,' declared Eli. 'It shouldn't be turned like that.'

'What do you want us to do, Boss?' asked Jed. 'Do

you want us to wait for the cattle drive? Only my rifle got swept away.'

'I lost mine as well,' said Eli, 'And yours is there, but it's all broken and bent.'

'Aagh! I've twisted my ankle. Get me down this cussed mountain,' growled Carter angrily, 'Get me back to Cedar Creek. You'll have to carry me!'

For a fleeting moment, Jed caught a glimpse of a large silhouette against the sky, and although it was unfamiliar and unexpected, there was something about it that stirred a memory. However, a billowing dust cloud swept in, veiling the mysterious apparition from sight, and he put it out of his mind. Dealing with his very irate employer was quite enough to think about!

'Well done, Jake, my man,' congratulated Oliver, 'It looks like they are retreating, tails between their legs.'

'Meeow! Beaten by a bloomin' pussycat!' sang out Billy happily, 'Can we get off back now? I've got beans to boil!'

CHAPTER FOURTEEN

Rooster leant back on his chair, patted his stomach, burped and smiled. He was a satisfied man.

'Johnny always treats us to breakfast at this hotel after we've got the cattle safely packed on the train and heading North,' Rooster explained to Billy. 'Once we got paid, there would be some of us who wouldn't leave the bar for a week!' Then he added wistfully, 'Still, that was in the days of horses. It didn't matter how drunk you were; your horse would find its way home. Now we have to walk it ain't to easy.'

'I must admit,' replied Billy, 'I woz gettin' fed up cooking beans wiv every bleedin' meal.'

'And I can't say I miss having all them cows for company. It's bad enough putting up with you lot!' laughed

Sadie as she looked around the saloon at the cowboys and the Rebel Runaways. Her eyes came to rest on Charlotte's. 'With certain exceptions, of course.'

'Charmin', I do declare,' exclaimed Billy.

'Anyway, Billy,' shouldn't you be seein' about the deed that Pete left you in his will?' Billy pulled a face.

'Oh, you should go,' implored Charlotte, 'He wanted you to have it. It would be disrespectful if you didn't.' Reluctantly, Billy pushed his chair away from the table and trudged out of the saloon.

Sadie was pleased Charlotte was with her because, once the cowboys had finished eating, the yarns and tall tales began.

'Oh, I've heard these a million times,' muttered Sadie with a roll of her eyes, 'And that's no exaggeration. Unlike some of the elaborate adventures they claim to have had.' She gestured towards a piano in the corner, empty beer glasses stacked next to an overflowing ashtray from the previous night resting on top of it. 'Play a tune for us, Charlotte.' The two girls went over to the piano. Charlotte played a few notes.

'Oh dear! It needs tuning. Forgive me, Herr Beethoven, it's been a while.' Sadie pulled up a chair, closed her eyes and listened as the music wafted over her, taking her to another place. Gradually, the chatter and laughter in the room died away as everyone listened to Charlotte play. After she finished, there was a hush for a few minutes before Rooster spoke:

'Well, I'll be damned. I didn't know all those notes were kept in that piano. It sure ain't like the tunes Fingers bashes out every night.'

'That was beautiful, Charlotte,' said Sadie, 'What was it called?'

'It's known as "The Moonlight Sonata". I'm afraid I played a few wrong notes. I could see if I remember some Mozart to play you. Perhaps "Lacrimosa". It's a bit sad though.' The room was still as Charlotte's fingers caressed the keys, everyone lost in their own thoughts. When she stopped, she looked across at Sadie and saw a tear rolling down her cheek. Charlotte pulled a leaf of sheet music from beneath a glass on top of the piano. 'I think we need something a little more lively,' she announced. This one has "Bright Tempo" written on it. I don't know it, but it's got lyrics, so if you are familiar with it, maybe you could help me out.'

Two bars into the tune, there was a roar of approval, and soon, every American in the room was singing along:

'I wish I was in the land of cotton; old times there are not forgotten,

Look away, look away, look away, Dixie Land.'

In fact, it was more a case of Charlotte accompanying the singers rather than the other way around. They made her play it three times and when she finished the room reverberated to cheering and applause. Just at that moment Billy swung open the saloon doors.

'Fanks very much indeed,' he beamed in delight, 'But I've only been away for 'arf 'n hour!'

Charlotte joined the others at the table.

'Did you get your title registered, Billy?'

'Well, it wasn't as bloomin' straightforward as all that,' replied Billy. 'It's all a right bleedin' palaver!'

'What do you mean?' asked Oliver.

'Well,' said Billy, shoving aside breakfast dishes to make some room and spreading a document out on the table, 'It says here that I am the legal owner of this land, but some uvver bleeder has bought it too, and he shouldn't have because my paper takes the president.'

'Precedent,' corrected Charlotte softly.

'That's wot I bleedin' said,' replied Billy, crossly. 'Wot's more, it says 'ere, that if Seb MacMurdy were to sell the land either side, then the owner of this strip of land 'as to have first dibs on buyin' it.'

'What's that? Did you say Seb MacMurdy?' asked Johnny, suddenly very interested. Billy nodded. 'So the Pete I've heard you talk about is his brother, Pete MacMurdy?'

'That's the fella. Why? Do you know 'im?'

'I certainly do,' replied Johnny, 'I was a youngster when Pete's pa died. Seb, God rest his soul, owned the spread next to our ranch. I always wondered what the two brothers quarrelled about.'

'I can see the logic behind what his father did,' commented Oliver. 'If you keep dividing a farm up between the children, the plot ends up smaller and smaller with each generation.'

'Yeah. The trouble was - it was the younger brother that got left the land, so that's why Pete was angry,' continued Johnny. 'Seb was the harder worker, though, until he took to the drink. But that was after he lost his wife in childbirth.'

'If I remember rightly,' pondered Oliver, 'The person who bought the land from Seb MacMurdy was...'

'Carter,' said Billy and Johnny together.

'The fing is,' continued Billy, 'The lawyer wot I saw said we would 'ave a case to get the land back and not only that, the judge will be in town tomorrow, so we could get the case added to the proceedin's. Carter is in town too apparently so he could be speenered.'

'Subpoenered,' whispered Charlotte.

'That's if we can be bleedin' bovvered,' Billy continued,

ignoring Charlotte's correction.

'Bothered!' roared Oliver, slamming his fist down on the table so hard it made the breakfast dishes dance.

'I was finkin' you might say that, so I got 'im to put our names on the list,' smiled Billy.

'It's damned short notice,' growled Carter at the judge, 'And a waste of my time.'

'Sir,' replied Judge Jackson, 'I am concerned only with upholding the law. I am sorry that you have had a long wait. You are the last case of the day, but at least you have had more time to prepare. I trust you are not in too much pain, Mr Carter.'

'Hrmph!' grunted Carter. Jake and Charlotte glanced at each other and smiled. They knew the reason why one of Carter's trouser legs had been slit to his thigh, revealing a heavily bandaged leg, and why two of his men, Jed and Eli, had carried him to the front of the room on a chair and positioned him next to his lawyer, Neville Holt. It wasn't a purpose-built courtroom; they were in the same room where the cowboys and the Rebel Runaways had eaten breakfast the previous day. The furniture had been rearranged, and Billy and Oliver were sitting at a table to the side of Carter, facing Judge Jackson.

Jackson peered over his glasses and looked at the plaintiff and defendant before him.

'Mr Carter and Mr Holt, I have met you on numerous occasions, and I am well aware of your growing influence in these parts, but erm...' The judge's voice tailed off as he surveyed Oliver and Billy in their outlandish garb.

'Oh dear!' whispered Charlotte to Sadie. Both Oliver

and Billy had insisted on returning to the airship to get changed out of their dusty clothes, which was a good thing, but despite Charlotte's advice, they had insisted on dressing in their extravagant finest, which, by the look of puzzlement on the judge's face, was not such a good decision. Of course, he had seen top hats before, but not ones decorated with bright, shiny cogs. He had seen colourful clothes before but usually worn by women, not by a young boy like the one before him who appeared to be wearing every colour under the sun. Even the complexity and profusion of the embroidery adorning the older man's jacket was surprising.

'We are new to the area, M'Lud, a flying visit, so to speak,' explained Oliver.

"Your Honour" is quite sufficient. Do I detect a British accent there?'

'Yes, Your Honour, and proud of it.' The judge scowled at Oliver. Then he heard someone whistling Yankee Doodle at the back of the room and banged his gavel down hard.

'Silence! These people may be foreigners, but I demand an orderly courtroom.'

Oliver was unperturbed by the animosity shown towards him, but Charlotte was worried.

'I wish he hadn't spent so long in the bar last night,' she whispered to Sadie. 'He said he was conducting research, but it looked like he was just laughing and chatting with the barman to me. I wanted him to have a clear head.'

Carter and his lawyer, however, were enjoying how the case was proceeding, so they nodded and smiled.

'The sooner we can throw these interlopers out of court, the better,' said Carter as an aside to Holt, but loud enough for the whole room to hear him. Many watching began to laugh. The judge once more rapped his gavel on the table, but did not reprimand Carter.

Judge Jackson scanned his papers for a few moments. Meanwhile, the onlookers tittered, enjoying seeing the British being put in their place. Oliver leant back in his chair and smiled complacently. Billy chewed his lip nervously and twiddled his thumbs. Finally, the judge looked up and addressed the room.

'So what we have here seems to be a simple case of an ownership dispute.'

'It's all nonsense,' declared Carter. His lawyer put a hand on Carter's arm to silence him and addressed Judge Jackson.

'Your Honour. My client bought the land in question above board, fair and square, and I have the documents here to prove it.' He waved papers in the air, and the judge gestured for them to be passed to him. Once again, the judge studied the paperwork. Billy was growing more and more anxious.

'Oliver!' hissed Charlotte, prompting Billy to look at Oliver. Discovering that he seemed to have fallen asleep, he gave him a gentle dig in the ribs. Oliver opened his eyes and smiled.

'Just resting my eyes, dear chap,' he murmured.

'So it appears according to this title that the plaintiff has been the legal owner of the land for three years, so I fail to see why he has a case to answer,' stated Judge Jackson.

'But that ain't wot should 'ave 'appened coz...' Now it was Oliver's turn to steady his client. Having previously been ambivalent about ownership of the land, Billy was now furious.

'Your Honour,' announced Oliver, 'With your

permission, might I look at the document that the plaintiff has passed to you?' The judge nodded and Oliver walked over to retrieve it.

'Go ahead and read it. Seb MacMurdy says in his own handwriting that he relinquishes all rights to the property, and that ownership is transferred to me!' shouted Carter.

'Relinquished,' repeated Oliver, 'There's a word that rolls off the tongue. Yes, it does say that here. In his own hand, you say.'

'Yes! It's there before you.'

'Your Honour, I presume you have seen the document left to my client, which states that the ownership of Seb MacMurdy's ranch had to be offered to his brother should it come up for sale.'

'I have, Mr Moon, but the deed states that all rights were relinquished and Mr Carter bought the land in good faith.'

'Relinquished,' murmured Oliver, 'There's that word again. Rather a tricky word,' and then looking at Billy, he added, 'You would think that there should be a "K" in it.'

'Ain't there?' asked Billy innocently. The half of the room who knew how to spell it laughed. Charlotte was annoyed that the onlookers appeared to be laughing at Billy.

'Your Honour, in the interests of justice, could I please call a witness to the stand?'

'I wasn't told you wanted to call a witness,' replied Judge Jackson tetchily.

'I didn't know myself until a few minutes ago. In fact, he doesn't know either!' said Oliver with a smile. The room erupted with laughter. Charlotte squirmed with embarrassment. Although Oliver was as polite and charming as ever, it wasn't quite the polished and expert performance she had been expecting.

'If you must!' snapped the judge, clearly irritated.

'Thank you, Your Honour. Can I please call Freddy 'Fingers' O'Malley to the stand?'

'There ain't no stand,' grumbled Carter. Oliver ignored the jeers from the spectators as the barman and sometime piano player stumbled, confused and concerned, to the front of the room.

'Do you swear to tell the truth, the whole truth, and nothing but the truth, so help you God?' asked Oliver.

'It's not in your remit to administer the oath,' groaned Holt. 'Amateur!'

'Apologies!' smiled Oliver as laughter rippled around the room.

'I do, Sir,' said Fingers, 'I'd swear on the Holy Bible, so I would.'

'Please tell the court how long you have known me.'

'I'd never seen hide nor hair of you before last night.'

'And we are not in collusion in some way?'

'In what?'

'A conspiracy. We haven't made a plan together?'

'God, no. I have no idea why I'm here at the stand, which isn't a stand.' Judge Jackson had to bang his gavel to quieten the laughter.

'Get on with it,' he growled.

'So sorry, Your Honour. Mr O'Malley. I take it that you knew Seb MacMurdy well?'

'Certainly,' replied Fingers. Someone from the back of the room yelled:

'He was never more than a foot away from your bar.'

'I've heard he liked a drink or two,' continued Oliver. 'Was that just since he sold the farm and had more time and money on his hands?'

'Oh no,' replied Fingers, 'He started to hit the bottle

hard after his wife and child died. Why, you would, wouldn't you?' There were murmurs of sympathy in the room as the crowd began to empathise with the late Seb MacMurdy.

'And did he ever speak of the sale of his land?'

'It was a constant complaint, and a worry too, because he had no recollection of it. One moment, he was a landowner, then the next he knew, he wasn't. He was drunk in this very room when someone told him, so he was. He was rarely sober after that day.'

'So, you think he was intoxicated when he relinquished the farm?'

'I do, Sir,' replied Fingers, nodding enthusiastically.

'Where is this going?' complained the Judge.

'So he couldn't hold his liquor. So what?' commented Carter.

'He was drunk when he relinquished the farm,' ruminated Oliver. 'Relinquished. That word again. Do you think old Seb would spell it with a "K"?' Fingers laughed.

'Old Seb? He couldn't spell it anyhow. He couldn't read and write.'

'Are you certain about that?'

'To be sure. I had to write several letters for Seb when he was trying to find if he had any kinfolk alive in the East. I wrote them, so I did, and he just scrawled an "x" at the bottom, and then I printed out his name.'

'I can vouch for that,' came a voice from the room, 'I run the store, and I had to order supplies for him.'

'Thank you, Mr O'Malley,' said Oliver, then turning to Carter, he asked, 'Any questions?' The plaintiffs were open-mouthed, trying to process the significance of this new information. Oliver turned to the judge. 'Your Honour, it appears that we have a dichotomy. On the one hand, you have before you a document allegedly signed by Sebastian MacMurdy, yet you have heard a witness testify that he could neither read nor write! Can I suggest, therefore, that the deed held by Mr Carter is not legal and that the document held by my client should take precedence?'

Judge Jackson took a moment to consider, banging his gavel to quiet the room before speaking:

'Mr Holt, do you have anything to say?'

'No, no!' replied Carter's lawyer, distancing himself. 'I wasn't representing my client at the time.'

'Mr Carter?' enquired the Judge. Carter shook his head angrily.

Cries of 'Shame on you!' echoed round the room. The gavel rang out once more.

'Then, Mr Moon,' replied the Judge calmly, 'I'm inclined to agree with you. Therefore, I declare Mr Carter's deed of sale null and void and reassign ownership of the land to your client. You will, however, have to recompense Mr Carter, who claims he bought the land in good faith for...' he glanced down at his papers, 'For a surprisingly small amount, considering its value.' The room erupted into cheers as the judge shouted, 'Here endeth this session of the court. Good day, gentlemen.'

DAVE JOHNSON

CHAPTER FIFTEEN

'Get me out of here!' yelled Carter to Jed and Eli. Fearful of their employer's temper, the two men rushed forward: each seized one side of Carter's chair and carried him out of the room. Carter was clutching a walking stick so tightly that his knuckles were white. He barely contained the impulse to lash out with it. The street was busy with people discussing the proceedings, and Carter heard the sound of laughter. People were laughing at him, and it was a sound that pierced him and stirred the boiling cauldron of anger within.

Jed was in turmoil, too. He hadn't quite understood how the Englishman had turned the mood of the room. Jed was used to being on the winning side and luxuriated in being employed by the most powerful landowner in the

County. This connection, combined with his skill with both fists and gun, meant that he couldn't remember the last time he had been beaten. He surveyed the scene ahead, then stopped dead, nearly unseating Carter. He set the chair down, Eli following his lead.

'What is it?' yelled Carter, 'Why have you stopped?'

'Well, I'll be...' Jed gazed into the distance, where he saw the silhouette of a large shape tethered to a tree. He pointed. 'What's that?' A young boy was skipping by and overheard him.

'I know what it is, Mister,' he said with an air of importance, 'It's an airship, and my Uncle has been paid a dollar to guard it - he's got a repeating rifle, you know. The airship belongs to the Englishman.' Then the boy ran off into the crowd.

Pictures flooded into Jed's brain. The time he had seen an airship for the first time tied up outside Rosa and Johnny's ranch. That hadn't been a successful day - a long walk for nothing. Then, there was something that he had never mentioned before because he did not know if it was a figment of his imagination. When they were caught up in the avalanche at Dead Man's Gulch, he thought he saw a large cigar-shaped object in the sky, but then it disappeared into the swirling clouds of dust. And now here it was again.

For some reason, Jed thought of his grandfather. Jed's father had been a violent and irrational man and Jed had learned to stay out of his way. He often sought solace in the company of his grandfather, who would regale him with tales of how the American nation was born and how, as a young soldier, he had helped to send the English packing. Now, before him on the street, laughing and chatting with his friends, was an Englishman celebrating winning a battle.

'Hey, Redcoat,' yelled Jed.

Oliver turned to face him, looking puzzled. He looked down at his embroidered jacket.

'You mean me?' he asked, 'Redcoat? I'd say this was rather an exotic shade of turquoise. Certainly not red.'

'Yeah, you, you...cowardly lobsterback,' Jed spat and hooked his jacket back to reveal a holstered gun. 'You might be fast with your mouth; let's see how fast you are with an iron.' Jed's hand twitched, ready to draw.

'Lobsterback? I can't say I've ever been called that before, and I've certainly never been called a coward. But, as you can see, my friend, I am unarmed.' Oliver opened his jacket wide to show that he did not have a weapon. 'Perhaps, Sir, if you could put aside your pistol, which would only hinder you, we might engage in a pugilistic encounter.'

'What?'

'Fisticuffs, my dear chap,' smiled Oliver, striking a boxing pose to demonstrate.

'I'll beat the living daylights out of you,' snarled Jed, unhooking his holster and throwing it at Carter's feet.

'Excuse me while I remove my not-very-red jacket,' replied Oliver, handing both it and his top hat to Jake. That enraged Jed even more, and he rushed at Oliver, swinging a fearsome punch. Oliver merely feinted to one side, stuck out a foot, tripping Jed, and sending him sprawling in the dust. The crowd quickly formed a circle. They were delighted to see Oliver toying with Jed - dodging his haymaker punches and landing gentle jabs at will, which served to infuriate Jed even more. At last, Jed realised that he had to change his tactics. The Englishman was too quick for him. Jed approached Oliver steadily, his fists at the ready, then suddenly he kicked out, surprising Oliver and connecting with his shin. Oliver grimaced in pain but evaded the punch that came his way.

'Oh, that's quite enough of that. This is getting a little tedious now,' Oliver exclaimed, and amid a quick flurry of punches to the solar plexus, Jed sank to his knees. Then, with one final right hook from Oliver he was knocked to the ground once again and lay senseless.

'Get up! Get up, damn you!' screamed Carter, struggling to his feet. Jed was in no condition to reply.

'Oliver!' shouted Charlotte in alarm. She saw that Carter was pointing his pistol at Oliver. The crowd gave a collective gasp, and then another woman's voice pierced the air. It was Sadie's.

'Put that gun down, or I'll kill you.' Carter barely glanced at the strangely dressed female wearing a single lace glove. Women did not figure largely in Carter's life in any capacity - neither for romantic reasons nor business. He mostly ignored them. Then, from behind, another voice reached him.

'You better bleedin' believe her, mister. She flamin' well means it.' Carter realised this was the boy who had caused all the aggravation - the one who now owned his land. Carter cocked the pistol, spun around and fired. However, in his anger, he had not taken into consideration that he had an injured leg and winced in pain, causing him to shoot wide of his target. A woman screamed and fell screaming, clutching her arm. Carter took aim once more at the transfixed boy. His shot rang out, but this time, the bullet flew harmlessly up into the air as Carter hit the ground with Sadie's dart embedded in his forehead.

'Well, you can't say I didn't bleedin' warn ya,' chirped Billy to the dead body, 'Fanks, Sadie. Can we go and get some nosh now? I'm starvin'?'

Oliver put his jacket on and, noticing that the judge

had witnessed the event, addressed him:

'A rather unhinged and desperate act of aggression, don't you think? Thankfully, he was stopped before causing any more harm. I shall pay the doctor's bills for that poor girl, and please witness the fact that if there are no beneficiaries to receive Carter's refund for the money he paid for the land, then I shall donate it to the town to found a school.'

'I think in the light of his actions, Sir, he has forfeited any entitlement to compensation. A school it shall be,' replied the judge.

'It's a good job that you have come to collect me,' laughed Joshua, 'Another day and I would be so fat that the Rebel would never get off the ground. Rosa has done nothing but feed me.'

'Well, a big boy like you needs to keep your strength up. Anyway, you've chopped up enough wood to last us through two winters, so you ain't exactly been lazy,' said Rosa. 'I'm glad you're back too, Johnny. I wasn't expecting you so soon.'

'I was keen to get back to tell you about Carter, so I jumped at the chance to get a ride in an airship,' replied Johnny.

'He was the only one, mind,' Sadie chipped in, 'The rest of 'em said they wanted to spend some time in the saloon, but I reckon they took frit.'

'I'd be happy to take you for a ride in the Rebel,' said Charlotte. 'You'll get a good view of your ranch from the air. And Billy's.' Rosa nodded enthusiastically.

'So, what kind of cattle are you going to have, Billy?

Texas Longhorns, or are you going to bring over some Jersey cows from Britain? You could even breed those hairy Scottish ones.' laughed Sadie.

'An you can bleedin' leave off an'all,' replied Billy indignantly, 'I ain't 'avin' any flamin' cows.'

'Actually, Billy and I have been discussing this,' chuckled Oliver. 'The land was relatively cheap. Carter took advantage of poor Jed while he was inebriated. So, we suggest that you farm the land, Johnny and Rosa, and pay me the money back over a period of, say, twenty years. Look at it as an interest-free loan. In the meantime, do what you want with it: bring the railroad through, establish a new town, make your fortunes.'

'I've got an idea how to make a few quid,' piped up Billy. 'Ave you ever thought about sellin' them bleedin' beans in tin cans? Proper tasty they are!'

'Well, that was an interesting distraction,' remarked Charlotte, 'But I suppose we had better get back on course. The tornado blew us in the wrong direction and then wrangling cattle took us even further from Savannah.'

'I know where we are now,' said Jake, unfurling a map. 'In the letter I found in Double Top's hotel room, he wrote about a meeting. I don't think we will be able to get there in time to confront him. It's too far from here.'

'Oh, that's a cryin' shame,' complained Billy.

'That doesn't mean we can't go anyway, does it?' asked Joshua, clenching his fists.

'Hell, no!' cried Oliver, characteristically banging his fist on the table. 'There'll be no hiding place for that scheming little snake!'

'By heck!' said Sadie, 'Before we set off, can we brew another cuppa? You've gone and spilt me tea wi' all your fist thumpin'!'

DAVE JOHNSON

CHAPTER SIXTEEN

'I've been told to report to you, Sir. My name's Matthew Strong.' Luke glanced at the soldier and nodded. He'd had several men transfer from regular units into the all-black regiment in which he served.

"This sassy young fellow is Corporal Isaac Thompson. You stick by him, and you won't go wrong. He's convinced he's invincible. Let me say that in a previous life he must have been a cat, because he always falls on his feet and he's got nine lives. Must have used some of 'em up by now, though.' Isaac grinned and held out his hand in welcome.

'You knows you are supposed to salute, not shake hands with Sergeant Strong!' reprimanded Luke, which made Isaac grin even more as he pumped Matthew Strong's hand.

Matthew found there were two types of people in the world. There were those who ignored the fact that his left ear was deformed and did their utmost not to be caught looking at it, and there were those who came right out and asked him about it. Isaac was definitely in the latter camp.

'Hey, brother. What happened to your ear? You been hit by too many right hooks? You gotta improve your defence...' Isaac proceeded to shadow box. Meanwhile, Matthew noticed that First Sergeant Luke Taylor was also staring at his ear, lost in thought. Finally, he spoke.

'Tell me, Sergeant, were you born in America?'

'No, I came here as a slave. I escaped and made my way North.'

'Do you remember where you landed?'

'I do,' replied Matthew, puzzled by this line of questioning, 'It was Savannah. Savannah, Georgia. I didn't know it at the time, but I stayed in that region a good while.'

'I was sold at the slave market in Savannah too,' said Luke. 'It was a long time ago, but I remember you. Or rather, I remember a young boy with a crooked ear sitting up on a cart next to my sister. That was the last time I saw her.'

'You mean Dorothy?' exclaimed Matthew, incredulously.

'I don't know her English name,' replied Luke, 'Just her African name.'

'I know that too,' said Matthew excitedly.

'What? You remember it after all these years?' asked Luke.

'Yes, because it's the same name as my Mother's.'

'Amara!' said Luke and Matthew simultaneously.

My dearest love, Jessy

I am writing this without any help so it will be short. I am happy because I met Matthew who knew my sister, and he thinks she may still live near Savannah. They were both owned by the same master until she was sent to a farm called "Rosebud". Matthew knows her African name which is Amara so I know he is telling the truth. Her name is Dorothy, now. If we get down as far as Georgia I will look for her.

Don't worry about me. Corporal Isaac watches my back and he says he is born lucky.

The quicker we can get this war finished, the sooner I can be with you.

All my love,
Luke

'COMPANY - FIX - BAYONETS!'

The massed Union troops looked nervous as the occasional artillery shell thudded into the field between them and the forest. They were safe for the moment because they were out of range, but they knew the Confederate forces were waiting for them, hidden in the trees. The drummer boys beat a steady rhythm, and the fifes played "The Star Bangled Banner."

'There sure is a lot of open ground between us and them trees,' muttered Isaac.

'Quiet!' reprimanded Luke.

'COMPANY - SHOULDER - ARMS!'

'Are we seriously going to walk straight up to them

graybacks while they is shootin' at us?' asked Isaac. A bugle sounded.

'There's your answer,' said Luke sardonically, then he shouted,'

'IN TWO RANKS- FORM COMPANY - LEFT, FACE!'

'I can't see why I am always in the front line,' grumbled Isaac.

'You know why,' replied Matthew, beside him. 'Firstly, you are a corporal, and the corporals are always in the first rank.'

'If I'd known that when they gave me my stripes, I would have said "No, thank you. Keep 'em!"'

'And secondly,' continued Matthew, 'You is a skinny little runt, and the smallest soldiers are always in front; otherwise, the line behind might blow the back of your head off.'

'So you are making it easy for them Johnny Rebs to blow the front of my head off!' protested Isaac.

'DOUBLE TIME - MARCH!'

'I heard tell that in the old days the cavalry boys would lead the charge seeking glory.' said Isaac as the two lines of Union soldiers began the long jog towards the enemy.

'Well, now the glory boys are all dead, it's your turn. The least you can do is keep in step,' said Luke.

'The way I see it,' replied Isaac, 'Is that if you've got a whole load of men doing the same thing and one doing something different, them Graybacks is gonna aim at the bigger target because it's easier.' Their conversation was abruptly interrupted by the deafening roar of an exploding shell, sending a plume of smoke up into the air and raining soil and turf down on them, momentarily obscuring their vision.

'Hell!' cursed Matthew.

'Probably looks like this,' quipped Isaac.

A few steps later, they saw puffs of smoke drifting from the trees, and several men in the line keeled over. Now, they were in range of the Confederate muskets.

'COMPANY - HALT!'

'If they can hit us, then we can fire at them,' said Matthew.

'They can see us, but we can't see them.' replied Isaac.

'COMPANY WILL FIRE BY BY RANK - REAR RANK - AIM - FIRE!'

Isaac winced as the back line of soldiers fired, almost deafening him; then he lifted his musket to his shoulder and fired into the trees at the same time as the rest of his row.

'COMPANY - QUICK MARCH!'

'I reckon we killed 'em all. We can go home now,' asserted Isaac. Matthew laughed, then as if in answer, another round of fire tore into the company, followed by cries and screams from injured soldiers. The air was thick with smoke now.

'I'm hit...' Matthew dropped to his knees, then flopped onto his front. Isaac faltered for a moment.

'Leave him, boy,' shouted Luke above the noise of battle, 'Nothin' you can do. Keep marching.'

'CHARGE!'

The Union soldiers ran towards the trees. Isaac was determined to reach cover as soon as he could, but it wasn't to happen. A round of grapeshot fired from the Confederate cannons decimated the frontrunners, and then a shell exploded just in front of Isaac, and he found himself blown off his feet, landing on top of Luke in a small crater.

'Sorry, I'll get off you,' panted Isaac. He rolled over and then looked in horror at his friend. 'Luke!' A dark stain was spreading over the Sergeant's tunic.

'I'll take you back to our lines,' cried Isaac, but Luke shook his head.

'It's over,' he said in a hoarse whisper, coughing blood as he spoke. 'If you get through this, can you take this to my Jessy?' Luke fumbled with his pocket and pulled out an addressed envelope. The corner was stained with fresh blood.

'If I get through this!' replied Isaac, 'You know I've got nine lives; I promise she will get it.' As Luke released the letter, he gave a brief smile, coughed, and then lay motionless as the life ebbed out of him. Isaac reached for his musket. He didn't know if it was damaged, but the bayonet was still fixed, and that would be all he needed to exact his revenge. Isaac scrambled to his feet, and with a scream that was so loud it surprised him, he ran towards the forest, intent on killing as many of the enemy as he could. Isaac had no fear, just rage. Then, the unexpected happened. Just as he entered the forest, first an explosion and then a loud creaking and tearing noise added to the turmoil. Isaac was unaware that a cannonball had crashed into a tree above his head. A second later, the tree crashed to the ground. Isaac was swallowed up beneath it, and all went dark.

Isaac groaned, then lay still as his head cleared and he tried to figure out where he was. The last thing he could remember was being in a battle, but it must be over now because it was too quiet. Not that it was silent, for he could hear indistinct conversations between men in the distance, and now and then, the sound of someone groaning filtered through to him. Who had won the battle? He was pinned to the ground by a tree. That much was obvious. Quietly, Isaac began to wriggle sideways. In doing so, his hand brushed against his musket; he grasped it and continued to extricate himself. At last, he was free and gingerly straightened up, only to find himself facing a Confederate soldier investigating the noises coming from the undergrowth.

Isaac instinctively raised his musket and pulled the trigger. He had no idea if it was loaded but was relieved when the roar from the gun and the surprised grunt from his target told him it was. One thing that Isaac had practised since that first day when he was on sentry duty was how to load his gun quickly. He took the wrap of gunpowder from his bag, tore it with his teeth and poured the contents into the muzzle. Then he rammed it down hard and loaded a ball. He could confidently load and fire his gun three times a minute and once more aimed it at a soldier emerging from the thicket. Then, as that man toppled, he saw four more arriving.

Isaac made a split-second decision. He could fight, he could surrender, or he could run. He was outnumbered, so he discounted the first option. The prospect of being a black prisoner in a Confederate jail was unimaginable, that is, if he made it that far alive. He was left with only one choice. He turned and ran.

A volley of shots rang out, but they all missed him. Isaac raced back across the field. The ground was littered with dead bodies, all wearing blue uniforms, and Isaac had to leap over them. Once, his foot caught on someone's leg, and he went sprawling. It was a fortunate mishap because he was aware of a round of bullets passing over his head as he fell. Maybe one of them would have hit him, but he had no time to count his blessings and was quickly up and running. He glanced behind him. His pursuers had stopped to fire and reload, but Isaac realised it would be a long time before he was out of range. Sooner or later, he would either tire and be captured, or else one of the soldiers would shoot him. Isaac looked to the sky as if beseeching God. What he needed was a miracle. Then one happened!

CHAPTER SEVENTEEN

'Take her five degrees to starboard, Charlotte,' said Oliver, 'I know what's been happening there. I'd like a closer look - but not too close. Don't take her any lower. I don't want any stray shots heading our way!'

'Goodness! That's horrific!' gasped Charlotte when she realised they were flying over a battlefield.

'Ee! The poor mite,' uttered Sadie, who was looking through a pair of binoculars. 'I can see a little drummer boy, and he's all shot to pieces!'

'It's a sad fact of war,' commented Oliver, 'Because different drum patterns are used to deliver messages to the troops, the drummers are often targeted.'

'Cor blimey!' cried Billy, 'They ain't all dead; there's someone running. E's bein' chased.'

'I see him!' said Oliver. 'He looks like a Union soldier. What to do? It's not really our war.'

'It reminds me of the day when we first met you, Joshua, running away from the farm,' said Charlotte.

'I'll tell you what else,' said Sadie, 'This chap's coloured as well, and also, he's waving his cap at us while he is running, trying to attract our attention.'

'So, do you think we should intervene?' asked Oliver, 'We could...' His suggestion was cut short because he saw that Joshua was already strapping himself into the harness.

'Get me down!' he commanded, then opened the gondola door and leapt out. Jake immediately rushed to the winch, waited for Joshua to stop swinging and spinning, and then engaged the clockwork gears to lower him.

Meanwhile, Oliver calmly gave Charlotte directions to move the airship directly in line with the running soldier, travelling towards him.

'The winch is fully wound out now,' called Jake.

'Then there is nothing else for it,' said Oliver, 'On my count, take her down, Charlotte. One, two, three!'

It went very smoothly, as though they had rehearsed the whole procedure. Charlotte slowed the airship down; the soldier stopped running, and then Joshua, who was travelling a few feet off the ground, slammed into him and wrapped his arms around him.

'Up, up up, as fast as yer bleedin' can!' yelled Billy. As it happened, the Confederate soldiers were so astonished that they didn't think to fire their muskets, and shortly afterwards, for the second time in his life, Isaac climbed aboard the airship Rebel.

'Isaac!' exclaimed the crew as he scrambled into the gondola and lay panting on the deck.

'I can't tell you how glad I was to see you come

floatin' by,' gasped Isaac, 'It was like an answer to my prayers. I always tell folk that I have nine lives, but to tell you the truth, I've lost count of how many I've got left.'

'It looks like your side had the worst of it,' commented Oliver, 'How come you were on your own? What happened?'

'I don't rightly know,' replied Isaac, pulling himself up to a sitting position. 'The last thing I remember was having an argument with a tree. The tree won, and when I woke up, the battle was over. I know my friend Luke got killed and...wait a minute.' Isaac searched through a pocket and pulled out an envelope. 'That's a relief. I was just checking I hadn't dropped it. I promised Luke I would get it to his sweetheart. I feel I know her already 'cause I helped Luke write some of his letters. Didn't write this one, though.'

'Maybe we could help,' said Charlotte, 'Where is it going to?' She took the envelope and read the address. 'It's going to Washington, the opposite direction to us, but we could drop it off on our way back.'

'Ee, poor lass,' said Sadie. 'If I were going to receive a letter from my sweetheart, knowing he was dead, I don't reckon I would want to get an envelope all covered in his blood.'

'You're right, Sadie,' replied Charlotte, 'I think we should open it and slip it into a new envelope.' Sadie slit the envelope open with a knife. 'We can respect his privacy and not read it,' Charlotte continued.

'Blow that!' exclaimed Sadie and proceeded to study it. 'Ecky Thump! This chap had just traced his sister to a farm called "Rosebud", and it's in Savannah, where we're going!'

'Can I come?' asked Isaac excitedly.

'Are you sure?' asked Oliver. 'You don't want to get shot as a deserter.'

'Luke and I were like the brothers we never had. He would want me to find his sister. Then you could take me back to a Union regiment, and I could say I was hiding, lost in the woods.'

'What's his sister's name, Sadie?' asked Oliver.

'It's Dorothy, and we know her African name too: Amara,' she said, checking the letter.

Oliver opened a window and bellowed at the top of his voice:

'Amara, we are coming to find you!' Then, gritting his teeth he muttered, 'And we're going to find you too, Double Top, I've a score to settle with you!'

'There it is, ahead of us,' announced Charlotte, 'Savannah!'

'About bleedin' time,' commented Billy, 'I'm lookin' forward to trying out some Southern nosh. The shrimps are s'posed to be good. Can't see them beatin' good old British cockles, but I won't know until I try 'em.'

'Can I remind you that whilst we are making our enquiries, we must keep a low profile?' said Oliver. 'So, Billy, that means that you are not to go flouncing into the top restaurants, dressed like a harlequin and asking the chef for recipes. And Joshua and Isaac, we have a few sartorial issues to resolve.'

'And what's that in plain English?' asked Isaac.

'Look at what you are wearing,' replied Oliver. Isaac looked down at his regulation Union army uniform.

'Well, all the best-dressed negroes in Savannah are wearing blue, but you have a point,' admitted Isaac.

'You too, Joshua,' added Oliver, 'I know that it will be an affront to your sensibilities now that elegance is your all-pervading standard…'

'There he goes with his fancy big words, again,' complained Isaac.

'But you have to blend in,' continued Oliver.

'You should 'ave a butcher's at your bloomin' boat race, Joshua,' laughed Billy.

'What?' asked Isaac, scratching his head.

'Dunno why you can't understand plain English. 'Ave a butcher's - butcher's hook - look, and boat race - face!' chirped Billy,

'It's true - you look like you're spittin' feathers, love,' added Sadie. In response, Joshua nodded his head morosely.

'Spitting feathers! Now, there's an interesting expression,' said Oliver. 'For some, it means they are angry, yet others interpret it as being thirsty. Which reminds me, it's been a while since I wet my whistle.'

'Don't even think about it!' warned Charlotte.

'Anyway, if we need some new clobber,' said Billy, 'Gimme the job of gettin' it.'

'Excellent!' replied Oliver, 'That's the spirit. Speaking of spirits, I've heard of this drink called Chatham Artillery Punch. It contains rum, whisky, brandy, champagne, lemons and sugar. Sounds delightful.'

'Oliver!' warned Charlotte in a low voice. Oliver winked and then clamped a hand over his mouth.

The bank clerk and Oliver stared at each other across the counter at the Planters Bank of Savannah. The clerk

narrowed his eyes as if thinking, and then spoke.

'You say you are looking for someone they call Double Top?'

'Yes, that's what I said,' confirmed Oliver, maintaining eye contact, 'I believe his real name is Topper.'

'Erm, I don't really recollect that name, Sir' replied the clerk. Excuse me, I'll go and ask my colleague.'

'He's lying,' said Oliver to Jake when the clerk retreated to an office behind the counter. 'He's playing for time.'

Inside the office, the manager, Cartwright, looked up with annoyance at Elliot, the clerk, who had entered without knocking.

'Sorry, Sir. There are two men outside asking for Double Top. Englishmen, I think they are. I told them I hadn't heard of him.'

'Are they now?' replied Cartwright and moved the blind on the door aside to get a better view. 'Tell them to come back in an hour while we find out where he is and send young Tommy in to see me. I've got an errand for him.'

Ten minutes later, Oliver and Jake were back out on the pavement, deciding where they should spend the next hour.

'Not enough time to walk back to the Rebel; I suggest a little drinkie at the nearest establishment,' said Oliver. Without Charlotte around to scold Oliver, Jake was powerless to stop him and he now strode off in the direction of the Marshall House in his quest for alcohol. Meanwhile, young Tom, the general dogsbody from the bank, was racing in the opposite direction, having memorised two messages. His first stop was a cheap saloon where he knew he would find Hunter. This was a man who operated just the wrong side of the law, but with the protection of the bank, and would provide tough and often lethal support when required. Tommy told him that Cartwright wanted to him to get over to Henderson's farm straight away and warn them to expect some unwelcome visitors. He would have an hour's head start. Next, Tommy ran to the luxurious Bay River hotel and knocked on the door of room seventy-two.

'Come in,' called Double Top. Tommy described the recent events. 'Did you see them? Can you describe them?'

'Well, Sir. They both had fancy clothes and wore bowler hats. One was tall and muscular. The other was smaller, and what was funny was that he was wearing gloves.'

'Hmm! Interesting. So they have followed me here, have they? I think Cartwright is more than capable of dealing with this. Thank you for the information. Here's fifty cents. Now, not a word to anyone, d'ya hear?'

The row of handcarts lined the side street, Beside each stood a slave waiting for his master. Jadon was not unhappy with his lot. As far as jobs went, this was a reasonable one. It was infinitely better than working out in the fields and better still than the experiences of those slaves the army had requisitioned to transport food, pull cannons and bring back the dead and injured. He could put up with the occasions when the handcart was loaded with heavy provisions and with his master, who appeared to be growing fatter by the day, perched on top. Jadon knew to make just the right noise every time his master flicked him with a whip - a little yelp to show that it hurt. He was always careful not to express annoyance or irritation and to momentarily quicken his pace before falling back to the same speed as before. Now, Jadon stared at the boy before him and laughed.

'I'm sorry, Sir, have I got this right? You gonna give me a dollar in return for clothes like mine? These rags?'

'Cor blimey, it ain't so boomin' difficult. That's right; one set at least as big as yours, and anuvver which can be a bit smaller,' replied Billy.

'And what you want the rags for?'

'None of your bleedin' business. D'ya want the flamin' dollar, or not?'

Jadon considered it for a moment and nodded. 'My master can't know about this. I'll get whipped if he finds out.'

'Don't you bleedin' worry, mate. Mum's the word,' said Billy, shaking Jadon's hand. Jadon wasn't altogether sure what the boy meant by that, but he liked his tone.

'You'll have to follow me when I take the master home. From a distance y'hear - y'ouse better not get seen. Half a mile from the plantation, there's a dead black tree that was struck by lightning. Wait for me there, and I'll come to you when I can.'

'Alright, Bob's Yer Uncle!'

'So disappear now, my friend,'

'Alright, keep yer hair on!'

Billy sat on the dusty ground and leaned against the blackened tree. Resting was not something he found easy, and he grew more and more impatient as he waited for Jadon to return. He flicked a dollar coin up in the air, caught it, and slapped it down on his wrist.

'Eads, 'e's coming, tails' e ain't.' Billy looked down at his wrist. 'Eads it is!' Then, as prophesized by the coin, he saw Jadon running down the track towards him.

'About bleedin' time!' complained Billy.

'What are you moaning about,' replied Jadon, 'You've just been lazing around. I had a wagon to unload.'

'I'm a busy man, fings to do, mate, fings to do. Show me what you got then!' Jadon laid the clothes out on the ground. 'They're just the ticket,' said Billy, tossing the coin into the air again for Jadon to catch.

Billy scooped up the clothes and then asked Jadon another question.

'I was wondrin', me old fruit, wevver you've ever 'eard of a place called Rosebud?' The expression on Jadon's face changed. One moment, he was delighted at having made a dollar for some useless rags that were due to be burnt because they belonged to a slave who had died; the next, he was wary and anxious.

'Er, no.'

'You don't flamin' look like you've never 'eard of it. I don't bleedin' well believe you.' Jadon looked at the ground for a few minutes before speaking.

'It's just that the Preacher said we should never speak of it.'

'You can tell me, mate. We're almost business partners.'

'Things are hard enough in this life. I don't want fire and damnation in the next!'

'Maybe I could go an' 'ave a word wiv 'im,' suggested Billy. Jadon snorted with laughter.

'Preacher Zacharias? He's a slave preacher. We meet in secret. They let us sit at the back of the regular white church sometimes, but these services are just for black folk. We've been reading "Exodus." He 'aint gonna talk to no white boy. He'll probably think it's a test or a trick. I'm sorry. I have to go now. I can't help you no more.'

CHAPTER EIGHTEEN

Sadie struggled to keep a straight face as she said goodbye to Joshua and Isaac. Neither of them looked happy to be wearing the ragged clothes that Billy had given them.

'I'll drop you off by the black tree,' said Charlotte, 'The plantation is a short walk from there; I saw it when I flew overhead whilst you were getting changed into your new outfits.'

Sadie burst out laughing. 'I'm sorry,' she said, 'By heck! You do look smart!' and once more began to giggle.

'Ignore her,' continued Charlotte, 'We are going to have to fly to Henderson's farm and watch over Jake and Oliver now. We'll come back to the tree to look for you as soon as we can.'

'Find Jadon. I'm sure he will lead you to the Preacher for another dollar,' said Billy.

The Rebel travelled at full speed and they arrived in time to see Oliver and Jake as they walked down the track towards Henderson's farm. Jake waved to acknowledge their presence. Now, they just had to keep watch and wait.

'I'm not sure about this,' fretted Jake, 'I know the bank teller said we wouldn't be expected, but I don't trust him.'

'Nonsense!' replied Oliver confidently, 'I have my sword stick. You have your dart-firing hand fitted and, of course, I have my remarkable and erudite command of the English language. What more can we need?'

'Well, all I can say is that I'm glad the Rebel is hovering nearby. We may have to make a hurried exit,' said Jake. Two men were digging in the vegetable patch outside the dilapidated farmhouse.

'Good afternoon,' said Oliver brightly, 'Rather chilly for the time of year, don't you think? What have you got there?' Oliver peered into a metal bucket at the man's feet.

'Taters,' replied the surly man.

'Ah! Jolly good. Apples of the earth, eh? I wonder if we might proceed to the farmhouse. We are making a few enquiries.' The man indicated with a nod of his head which direction they should head in. 'Excellent! Lead the way, shall we? In the vanguard, so to speak, eh.' There was no reply from either of the two men, who each picked up their shovels and followed Oliver and Jake to the farmhouse. 'I don't suppose you could tell me if Double Top is at home, could you?'

'Nope.'

'No, he's not in, or no I won't tell you,' wondered Jake.

'I'll go in, shall I?' enquired Oliver pleasantly, receiving only a sullen nod in response. Oliver pushed open the door and he and Jake entered the house, followed by the two men. There was a large room with a table at the centre and a log fire burning in the hearth. Beyond, there was another room, presumably a kitchen, and Jake and Oliver could hear sounds coming from it. 'Hello! Oliver Moon at your service; I would be very grateful if you would be so kind as to...' His words were cut short as, in unison, the two men swung their spades, making contact with the back of Oliver and Jake's heads, and the two Rebel Runaways slipped into unconsciousness.

'What should we do now, Ma?'

'Tie 'em to a chair,' said a woman adjusting her apron strings as she came through from the kitchen. 'When they come to, we'll find out what they know. Then you'll know what to do with 'em. In the meantime, you can start digging.'

Three pairs of binoculars were trained on the farmhouse.

'Cor blimey, they seem to 'ave been in there a long bleedin' time!' said Billy.

'I know,' agreed Charlotte, 'Oliver said he would make an excuse about needing some fresh air and come to the door to blow his nose. If he uses his white hanky, he's alright; if he uses his red one, he senses danger. But what if he doesn't come to the door at all?'

'Then we'll come knocking,' said Sadie, fitting the Glove on her hand.

'I'll tell you what's bloomin' odd,' commented Billy,

'Them geezers what were digging took their spades inside but left the spuds behind. 'Old up, here they come. They've got their spades; maybe they ain't finished. No, wait on. They are walking furver away. What's their game, then?'

Billy watched the two men digging whilst Charlotte and Sadie studied the farmhouse.

'I'm flamin' well not likin' this,' muttered Billy, 'They are diggin' it too bleedin' deep for vegetables!'

'Goodness!' said Charlotte, it looks the same size as...'

'A grave,' finished Sadie. 'That's it! We are going down there.'

Joshua and Isaac set off walking towards the plantation. Joshua decided to keep to himself that he had noticed something grim and ominous when he had looked up at the black tree. He knew the tell-tale signs. Approximately ten feet from the ground, a rope had rubbed a bough to a shiny patina. It was a hanging tree!

'It's alright for you; you are on familiar territory, but I ain't ever been a slave,' complained Isaac.

'Ignorance is bliss,' replied Joshua, 'I have no desire to return to those days.'

As they passed through the trees, they saw several long, wooden buildings. Beyond the huts was an imposing three-storey house, surrounded by manicured lawns.

'Duck behind here,' whispered Joshua. 'There will be twenty or thirty people living in each of them. Everybody will know everyone. They are sure to know Jadon and the Preacher.' Joshua and Oliver crept up to the first hut and tried the door. It swung open, and to their surprise, they soon found it was empty. It was the same when they investigated the next hut.

'Hush! Listen! You hear that?' asked Joshua, picking up the rhythmic percussive beat. Drawn by the sound, they found themselves in a clearing, where slaves were shuffling anticlockwise around in a circle. The noise they had heard was the sound of hand claps and foot stamping. The slaves sang in a call-and-response fashion.

'Move, Daniel, move, Daniel.
Move, Daniel, move, Daniel.
Oh, Lord, pray, sinner, come,
Oh, Lord, sinner gone to hell.
Move, Daniel, move, Daniel,
Move, Daniel, move, Daniel.'

'It's a ring. A ring shout,' whispered Joshua. They might go on like this for hours. Then, a man held up his hands, and one by one, the dancers stopped.

'It is time I returned home. It's a long walk. I have some valuable words from the scriptures for you - from Exodus:

I am the LORD, and I will bring you out from under the yoke of the Egyptians. I will free you from being slaves to them, and I will redeem you with an outstretched arm and with mighty acts of judgment. I will take you as my own people, and I will be your God.'

'That's our man,' said Isaac softly, 'We'll follow him when he leaves.'

The congregation gathered around the Preacher and said their goodbyes. Eventually, he was able to leave, and he made his way down a track through the forest, accompanied by one of the slaves who held on to his arm. Joshua and Isaac circled around to intercept them.

'Excuse me, are you Preacher Zacharias?' asked

Joshua.

The two men stopped and stared at Joshua and Isaac.

'We want to ask you a question,' added Isaac.

The Preacher and his companion noticed different things about the men who stood in front of them. Zacharias listened to their voice patterns. In Joshua, he could hear inflexions that indicated that he was of African descent but had once lived in the Southern states, although his voice was infused with a more cultural tone. He could tell that the other man, whilst obviously an American, was clearly from the North.

'I've seen that shirt before!' exclaimed Jadon, 'I recognise that patch on the sleeve.'

'Ah!' said Joshua, 'Then perhaps it was you whom our fellow traveller, Billy, bought these clothes from.'

'Well, I'll be...' Jadon's voice trailed off as he couldn't think of a suitable word to say in front of the Preacher.

'I reckon you should be paying us a dollar to wear them,' said Isaac, and then to Zacharias, he added, 'I don't suppose there's something in the Bible about not judging people by the clothes they wear?' Jadon laughed.

'The Preacher ain't bothered about the clothes you're wearing. He's blind! That's why I'm guiding him home.'

'What did you want to ask me, child?' said Zacharius.

'Simply this. We want to know how to get to a farm called Rosebud.'

Before anyone had a chance to speak, the air was filled with the sound of shrieks and shouts punctuated by a dog barking.

'The Master's men are breaking up the meeting. We must leave!' said Jadon in alarm.

'You three go, I'll catch you up. I'll wait a while to see if I need to delay them,' commanded Joshua.

Zacharius, Jadon and Isaac disappeared into the forest whilst Joshua remained, crouched at the ready. Then suddenly, a man with a snarling bulldog straining at the leash appeared. The man slipped the dog off its leash, and it came hurtling towards Joshua and leapt at him. It was a heavy, forceful brute, and it would have knocked most men over, but Joshua managed to grip the beast around the neck and fling it into a bush, where it scrambled to its feet and cowered, growling at him, a little more wary now. When Joshua turned to face the dog handler, he discovered that three more men were advancing, each with a musket trained on him.

'Well, lookee here, we just bagged ourselves a Preacher,'

'I've got an idea,' said Billy, 'Set me down on the roof, quickly, while those flamin' grave diggers' 'ave their backs turned.'

'I'm coming with you,' said Sadie firmly. A few minutes later, they alighted softly on the farmhouse roof. Billy was clutching one of Joshua's tartan cloaks.

'What have you brought that for?' Sadie hissed, 'Joshua will be right mardy when he finds out.'

'He'll be even narkier when he finds out what I've done wiv it,' whispered Billy. Then, bundling the cloak into a ball, he stuffed it into the mouth of the chimney pot. 'This'll bring 'em out!' It took around five minutes before the front door burst open and three men and a woman tumbled out, coughing and spluttering followed by a billowing cloud of smoke.

'I wonder if there's a back door?' pondered Sadie, and she edged down the rear slope of the tin roof and peered over. There was, and she grasped hold of the rope ladder that dangled from the Rebel and tossed it over the side. 'I'm going in the back way,' she said to Billy, thinking that it was a pity there wasn't something at the front of the farmhouse to distract the former occupants. She could hear them arguing about who should go back inside to investigate the cause of the smoke. She didn't expect Billy to cause the diversion; for that matter, neither did Billy! He sat down beside the chimney, and then, for the second time in his life, he found himself sliding down a roof. The last time he had been saved by guttering, but there was no such luck this time. However, whereas the Steam Works had been a very high building, the farmhouse was only single-storey, and he was also fortunate to have his fall broken. That is to say Billy was thankful; Hunter, the man he landed on was not so pleased!

'Take him inside!' commanded the woman, 'And throw some water on the fire, for God's sake!' Hunter grabbed Billy and pushed him forcibly into the farmhouse. He grabbed a pail of water from the veranda then strode inside, keeping one eye on Billy, and threw the water on the fire, extinguishing it with a hiss of steam. Hunter didn't expect the kitchen door to open and to see a figure silhouetted in the doorway. He reacted quickly. There was a loaded musket leaning against the wall, and he leapt over to it and raised the gun to aim at the intruder. Whether he would have taken such action had he known he had been surprised by a woman no one would ever know because Sadie's dart pierced him between his eyes, and he died instantly. His musket clattered harmlessly to the floor.

Although shaken by his recent tumble, Billy acted

swiftly. He closed the front door without making a sound and dropped the bar into place to secure it. Sadie had quickly scanned the scene, dashed into the kitchen and returned with a sharp carving knife. She realised that Oliver was conscious and cut the ropes that bound him to the chair.

'Bravo!' he smiled, then winced and held the back of his head where it hurt. When Sadie freed Jake, he slumped over, still insensible.

'Quick, out the back, Oliver. Can you carry Jake?'

'My pleasure. Onward!' replied Oliver.

Billy led the way, carrying the discarded musket. He peered through the back door to check the coast was clear before he left followed by Oliver, who, despite his own injury, carried Jake over his shoulder. Finally, Sadie, with her Glove at the ready, edged backwards out of the farmhouse.

Oliver spotted a pail of water beside the back door, so he set down his load and threw the bucket's contents over Jake, who spluttered into life.

'I do apologise, my young friend, but it's time we took our leave, and it would be altogether more convenient if you could climb up the rope ladder unaided.' Jake nodded weakly. Then, turning to Billy, Oliver said, 'And pray, what do you intend to do with that musket? Have you joined the infantry?'

'Nah! One fewer gun that could be fired at me. Takin' bleedin' liberties, they are. I don't suppose we could sneak round the front, could we? I couldn't 'elp noticin' there's a bucket full of spuds that would be proper tasty mashed up wiv some sausages!'

CHAPTER NINETEEN

'I hope we haven't been too long,' said Charlotte, 'The black tree is at the end of this track, just around the bend.'

'Yes, I'm afraid things didn't exactly go to plan,' commented Oliver, rubbing the bruise on the back of his head.

'Plan? I was never aware there was a plan!' complained Jake, pressing a wet towel against his bruised scalp.

'Now, now, boys. Let's concentrate on the matter at hand - picking up Isaac and Joshua and then finding this place called Rosebud. We can return to finding Double Top later.'

'Cor blimey! Over there! Ain't that Isaac?' exclaimed Billy, pointing at a dark-skinned man waving his shirt above his head to attract their attention.

'Yes, you're right!' cried Jake, 'He must be in trouble. Slow down, Charlotte. I'll lower the harness. I can't see Joshua, though.' All thoughts of self-pity evaporated; he was no longer aware of his painful bruise. It was time for action.

Onlookers gasped as Joshua tried to adjust his position, and the wooden crate he was standing on wobbled precariously. The overseer and his hands laughed and sniggered. It had been difficult to climb to the top of the three upturned boxes, made more challenging because his hands were tied behind his back. Joshua was no longer wearing his newly acquired slave shirt. The overseer had ripped it from his back before he had been tied to a post and whipped. From the moment that he was captured, Joshua had not said a word. He had borne his flogging without uttering a sound. Now, although the assembled slaves could see the blood dripping from the ugly welts on his back, they were mostly focused on the noose drawn tightly around his neck.

'Let this be a final warning to you,' cried Kluger, the plantation owner, 'We have forbidden you from carrying on that mumbo-jumbo abomination of our precious religion, and this is the consequence. Your so-called priest will begin the journey down to hell before your eyes. This creature is nothing more than a subservient rebel. Did he turn the other cheek like a man of the cloth? No! He viciously assaulted my men, and now he will pay the price.'

Half a mile away, just around the bend in the road, the Rebel Runaways were feverishly working. Jake, as always, had been busy on the journey to Savannah and modified the net they had used to scoop up the submersible, and later, to transport the chuck wagon on the cattle drive. He had used his little clockwork tadpoles in the sea to widen the net. To pick up the chuck wagon, Charlotte had hovered overhead whilst Billy spread out the net, but then there had been no hurry. Convinced he could automate the procedure, Jake was now enjoying the fruits of his labour. As the Rebel sped along, following the road, Oliver was standing at the base of the net, strapped to a harness, watching clockwork telescopic rods extend to create a rigid structure. As the Rebel rounded the bend, they were travelling at full speed, and Oliver was just a few feet above the ground.

At the hanging tree, Kluger had instructed all the slaves to file past Joshua, look him in the eye, and be warned that next time, it could be one of them balanced on a box with a noose around their neck. They weren't permitted to speak, but Joshua could see tears rolling down the cheeks of slaves who had never seen him before. They didn't know who he was, but they recognised that his silence was a means of protecting Preacher Zacharius. Joshua stared resolutely into the distance. The nearest slave, looking up at Joshua, thought it was curious that Joshua's mouth had curled up into a smile. Then, Kluger and his men were astonished to see the slaves scatter in all directions.

'Get back here! You'll pay for this!' yelled Kluger.

The overseer glanced over his shoulder and saw the airship bearing down on them.

'Boss!' he cried, wrestling his employer to the ground. Kluger roared in annoyance, his white suit now stained yellow by the dusty road as the Rebel sailed above their heads. The cables connected to the net struck the uppermost branch of the hanging tree, but momentum kept the net swinging towards the condemned man. Joshua was a little anxious because he could see that Oliver, supported by his harness, was leaning with his sword outstretched in the manner of his earlier incarnation as a cavalry officer. The net made contact with the boxes supporting Joshua, knocking them flying, but before Joshua fell into the net, Oliver had already swung his sword and severed the rope above Joshua's head. If there hadn't been so much screaming, Billy might have been heard shouting from above:

'Got 'im. Let's get out of 'ere!' In a complicated manoeuvre to ensure the net swung clear of the tree, Charlotte took the airship up and away from the stunned crowd.

'I say! That was tremendous fun. Can we do it again?' purred Oliver.

Charlotte paused at the plantation. Where better to fold the net back up than on the lawn in front of Kluger's house? After all, everyone, including his wife and children, was at the hanging tree.

'Do you still have the paint that you used to put numbers on the Air-Fleet airships for the lottery?' asked Joshua. Jake nodded. 'Then, before we fold up the net, Charlotte, can you take me high up alongside the house wall? I may not be a Preacher, but I know my Bible. I worked for a minister once; in fact, he taught me to read.'

Twenty minutes later, when the hanging party arrived back at the house, they were astonished to see the message daubed high on the house wall.

"There is neither Jew nor Greek, there is neither slave nor free, there is neither male nor female; for you are all

one in Christ Jesus.
Galatians 3:28"

'I still say we should 'ave gone back fer them bleedin' spuds,' complained Billy, 'You'll just 'ave to 'ave bread wiv your sausages!'

'That will be perfectly alright, Billy, my boy,' said Oliver, 'It's jolly nice to have us all together around one campfire. Cheers!' He pulled out the stopper from a bottle of whisky and took a swig.

'Oliver!' scolded Charlotte, 'Where did you get that from?'

'Ah! I keep a bottle put by. Purely for medicinal purposes; I had a bang on the head, you know.'

'Well, I think that's quite enough self-medication, thank you very much!' Charlotte held out her hand, and Oliver reluctantly placed the bottle in it. 'Sore head or not, you need a clear head. We're not finished here!'

'By heck, it's been one step forward and two steps back! Have we got anywhere?' said Sadie.

'It's time I made an announcement,' said Isaac. 'I know where to find Rosebud.'

'What! How?' exclaimed Joshua, 'Nobody told me.'

'When the Preacher heard you had stayed behind to create a diversion while they escaped, he said that Jadon should tell me. Jadon wouldn't say much; they think it is bad luck to talk about it. He said good is born of evil there; he told me there would be an armed guard. The farm isn't called Rosebud at all. That's just a nickname. Jadon described the landscape. I reckon if I looked at a map, I could find it.'

'Then I suggest we get a good night's sleep and go there first thing in the morning. Nightcap, anyone?' said Oliver, pulling another bottle of whisky from his jacket pocket. Charlotte rolled her eyes and sighed.

As the sun crept over the horizon, the Rebel flew towards the low-lying building. They had risked a pass over it at a high altitude, and through his binoculars, Jake meticulously surveyed the scene, pinpointing the veranda overlooking the road and a drowsy looking guard reclining in a chair. They couldn't see any doors at the rear of the property, and the windows along the side were small, barred and high up. It was obvious that the Rebel Runaways would have to gain access via the front. Now, however, they approached from the rear, where they hoped they would be unobserved.

'I can't see why I can't come along,' complained Joshua.

'I know you are courageous, Joshua,' said Oliver firmly, 'But those brutes flogged you severely, and you are still weak and feverish. You might be a liability; in any case, I don't want to leave Charlotte alone in charge of the Rebel. Someone will need to operate the winch.' Joshua nodded reluctantly.

This time, there was more of a plan than when they had visited Henderson's farm. That was because Jake had taken charge. On his command, Charlotte expertly lowered the net once more and set down Jake, Oliver, and the Chucky-Scoot that Billy had used to transport provisions when they were on the cattle drive. Oliver was the last person Jake would trust to steer a monoscoot, which was why Oliver lounged in its trailer whilst Jake engaged the clockwork motor and sped towards Rosebud. Suppressing speculation about why Preacher Zacharius labelled Rosebud as "evil," Jake focused on their mission.

He halted outside the back of the building, and Oliver climbed off the trailer. Even in the dim, early-morning light, Jake could see that Oliver had a glint in his eye, and that his mouth was twitching, suppressing a smile at the thought of what was to come.

Oliver crept round to the right and Jake to the left, pausing at the veranda, which stretched the full width of the wooden building.

They had no idea if the guard was awake or asleep, but Jake intended to wake him in a way only he could. Jake was never idle when travelling in the airship; one of the things he had created on the journey to America was nestling in his pocket, and he intended to use it. Jake had adapted one of his earlier inventions. He had used the Spider to cut a hole in the deck of the Deception when they were in Africa. He had christened it the Cockroach because it was virtually indestructible. It did little more than run around in circles until its clockwork motor ran out, but that was enough. He activated the switch underneath the Cockroach and, keeping out of sight, rolled it along the veranda's decking, then stepped back into the shadows and waited.

The guard had been asleep, but the noise of Jake's clockwork plaything scuttling noisily around the deck roused him from his slumbers. If there was one thing that Enoch, the guard, hated, it was a cockroach. At first, he recoiled in horror; then, seeing the insect mindlessly running around, he crept towards it and stamped on it.

'Got you!' he exclaimed, raising his foot to reveal the flattened creature. To his surprise, six legs and an antenna protruded from its shell and it dashed a few feet away and carried on as before. Once again, he brought his foot down on it with full force, and then, after a few seconds, the whole sequence was repeated.

'I'll show you,' growled Enoch, and he retrieved his musket from beside his chair, took aim, and fired. He didn't care if he woke all of Rosebud's inhabitants. After all, they were only slaves!

Inside, the noise was greeted with alarm, which was echoed by Isaac, Sadie and Billy, now stationed behind the building. Jake winced; he wasn't sure if his invention could withstand the force of a musket ball! Oliver, however, was pleased to hear the gunshot because it meant the guard now had an unloaded weapon. Oliver had been watching Enoch's antics with glee and now vaulted over the balustrade and swiftly approached the guard who was staring at the hole he had made in the floor. It was not in Oliver's nature to attack anyone from behind, so he tapped Enoch on the shoulder.

'I say! If you would be so good as to turn around…' As Oliver expected, the guard did as requested, and then, with a single and powerful punch to his chin, Oliver duly ended the guard's shift on duty. 'The coast is clear, Jake,' he called. Jake relayed the information to Isaac and Sadie, who joined him and Oliver on the veranda. Meanwhile, Billy waved a handkerchief to signal to Charlotte and Joshua that all was going to plan.

'I would have thought the noise from that gun would have brought any other guards rushing out, so I presume he is here alone,' said Jake.

'Then the place is ours.' Oliver, beckoned towards the

door. 'My fellow Runaways, after you.'

Jake drew back the bolts on the door.

'It was locked from the outside,' he said. 'So it's clear they didn't want anyone to leave.' He pushed the door open to reveal a long corridor with doors on either side. They couldn't see anyone, but they could hear a woman moaning at the far end of the passage.

'What is this place?' gasped Sadie as she hesitated in the doorway. 'It's like a prison.' Isaac was in no mood to be reticent, and remembering why they had come, he strode down the corridor, shouting, 'Dorothy...Amara...Dorothy...Amara,' over and over again. Slowly a door opened and a young black girl emerged.

'Why are you shouting my Mama's name?' she asked. Three more children, younger than her, crept out from behind her skirts.

'Amara is my Mama's name,' said a small boy.

'Her brother wanted me to find her,' said Isaac gently. 'Can I see her?'

'I didn't know she had a brother,' said the first girl. 'She's sick. That's my Mama you can hear.' Sadie wavered no longer and rushed down the corridor towards the moaning sounds. Undeterred by the prospect of danger She burst through the far door. She quickly took in the scene before her, then turned and blocked the door.

'You can't come in here, Isaac,' she said firmly, and closed the door.

There were two black women in the room; the first, who was elderly and plainly startled by Sadie's arrival, stood aside to reveal the second woman, who was lying on a wooden bedstead. There was no mattress, but the sheet covering her was stained red with blood.

DAVE JOHNSON

CHAPTER TWENTY

'Who are you?' asked the older woman, 'Where's Enoch? What do you want?'

'My name's Sadie. Who's Enoch? Is he the guard?' Sadie received a nod in reply. She glanced at the table in a corner of the room, then quickly turned away at the sight of something small and bloody wrapped up in cloth. 'We tied Enoch up on the veranda. We've come to rescue Dorothy.'

'She can't be moved. I fear the only person coming to rescue her will be the Good Lord Jesus.'

'Can she hear me?'

'I don't rightly know.' Sadie moved over to Dorothy's side and took her hand.

'Dorothy. Amara,' she whispered, 'Your brother wanted us to come to take you away.' Sadie racked her brain to remember what Luke's African name was. Isaac had told her. Then she heard Amara say in a weak voice:

'Kambi,' Then she squeezed Sadie's hand and said, 'My children. Who will protect them?' Amara gave a long, raspy breath, shuddered and then was silent. Sadie paused a moment and then gently closed Amara's eyes.

'What is this place, this Rosebud?' asked Sadie.

'That's just a name they use to make it sound sweet,' said the woman bitterly, 'Ain't it obvious? It's a breeding farm, and I'm the midwife, Dolly. The midwives at Rosebud are always called Dolly.'

'How many children has she got? We met four of them.'

'Yes, four of them here at Rosebud. Maybe another three have been sold and are working the fields.'

'How many children are there here?'

'Twenty-three, I think,'

'And how many mothers,'

'There's only another three. Clarrie is due in a month. Freda has a six-week-old baby, and there's a young girl called June who is next in line.'

'It's barbaric!' cried Sadie, 'You've all got to come with us.'

'You better ask the others. I ain't going. Who is going to help the poor girls still to come?'

'Then we'll burn this building down!'

'You think that's gonna stop it?' said Dolly, shaking her head sadly, 'They will only start again somewhere else. It's a profitable business. They even sell bonds backed by the value of these slaves. At least this is a decent building. Not like some I've worked in.'

'Are you alright in there?' called Isaac. Sadie opened the door and nodded.

'Consider your promise has now been carried out. It's too late for Amara, but we've got children to rescue.'

'You are gonna have to be quick!' said Dolly. 'They are gonna be bringing in some new stock this morning, including a new stockman, because the last one tried to escape, so they shot him. Although Double Top often likes to do it himself, 'specially when it's a young new girl.'

'Double Top?' gasped Sadie.

'Yes. He owns Rosebud.'

Just then, Billy came racing down the corridor.

'The flamin' guard's escaped,' he yelled.

'How?' demanded Oliver. I tied him up!'

'He told one of the kids to use his knife and cut him free. He said the boy's Mum would be punished otherwise. These kids are used to doing whatever the white man bleedin' well tells 'em.'

'Ah, well. It can't be helped,' said Oliver nonchalantly. 'Let's see who wants to come for a ride.' Although Oliver sounded calm, Sadie noticed he was clenching his fists, whether because of the prospect of meeting Double Top or because he might miss the chance of a confrontation with his adversary, she didn't know.

'Come on, Oliver,' she said, trying to distract him. 'Go and get the children to line up. Start with Amara's - they are definitely coming with us. I won't let anyone send them out to work in the fields.' Then Sadie realised she was clenching her own fists.

The next fifteen minutes were chaotic:

'How are we gonna escape? They'll use dogs to track us down. I ain't going.'

'You'll be flying out of here. Dogs can't track a scent that high up.'

'I can't go. I've already got three children working in

the fields.'

'How do you know they won't have been sold on by the time you get out of here? How old are you, June?'

'I'm thirteen. It all sounds too scary.'

'You're still a virgin; you gotta go. They're gonna expect you to have ten chillun by the time you are twenty.'

'But they said I could go free.'

'And you believe them, chile?'

'I'm nearly due.'

'I know, Clarrie, there's a risk, but look what happened to poor Amara!'

In the end, every single person except the midwife agreed to join the Rebel Runaways. The first group left the building. Billy brought the mono-scoot to the veranda; the heavily pregnant Clarrie lay on the trailer, and her children followed them to the airship, where they climbed into the net. Joshua, glad to be of use at last, winched them up into the Rebel along with the scooter. Billy ran back to see if he could be useful. He stopped dead in his tracks and peered into the distance, then raced inside to warn the others:

'Double Top! I can see people. I bet it's Double Top. They're only a hundred yards away; we've got to get out of here!'

'Oh no!' gasped Jake. They will see us leaving. I don't think we've got enough time to take everyone to the Rebel and get up in the air to safety!'

'If only there were another way out!' complained Sadie.

'There is,' said Amara's son, who was determined not to miss out on an adventure. 'We can go out of the trapdoor.'

'The what?' exclaimed Sadie.

'It's a secret trapdoor,' explained June. 'The children sometimes use it to sneak out and steal fruit when it's in season.'

'Then why don't you use it to escape?' asked Sadie.

'And go where?'

'Will you stop with all the chatting and just go!' yelled Isaac, 'I'll hold 'em off!'

'I'll join you,' said Oliver. 'I prefer fisticuffs or using a sword, but I know how to load a musket.'

'You load, I'll fire,' called Isaac over his shoulder as they raced to the veranda. 'We've got three guns - mine, the guard's and the one Billy got from the Hendersons.'

'How beautifully ironic it would be if I were to shoot Double Top with a gun belonging to one of his men,' replied Oliver.

'They are not in range yet,' said Isaac as he aimed his musket over the side of the porch rail. 'Join me for the first shot, then after that, you are on loading duty.'

'Yes, Corporal. Don't you know I was an officer?' laughed Oliver.

'Not in America, you ain't. You're in my army now, and I outrank you here. Ready, fire!' Both men whooped with delight at the sound of gunfire, first theirs, then the reply. The battle had begun!

Meanwhile, inside, the exodus was in full swing. Amara's son had pulled back a frayed old rug and lifted several floorboards, revealing their escape route. Billy followed him through the narrow opening, and they crawled to reach an air vent, which they forced open.

'Cor blimey, It's a bit of a bloomin' squash,' yelled Billy.

'I'm not going down there!' asserted Sadie. 'I'm not getting me petticoats all dirty. Billy, you and Jake lead them to safety. I'll go out the front way with Isaac and Oliver.'

'You could help me put the boards back,' said Dolly,

who was still determined to stay. 'We may as well keep this way out a secret.'

On the veranda, Isaac lay at full stretch on the floor so as to present less of a target, knowing he would not have to straighten up to reload. Oliver was efficiently carrying out that duty, sitting with his back to the wall and whistling as he rammed home gunpowder into the muzzle of each musket and loaded the lead balls. After Isaac felled the first of his targets, the others quickly hid behind a rocky outcrop and fired blindly at the building. Isaac's bullets were landing so close to them, ricocheting off the rocks, that they dared not show their faces for long.

'We are getting a little low on ammunition, old chap,' warned Oliver, 'Maybe you should slow down. We don't know how long it will take for everyone inside to escape.'

'I can answer that,' said Sadie, appearing in the doorway, 'Apart from Dolly, who won't leave, they've all gone through the trapdoor now. I'd say they will need another fifteen minutes to get aboard the Rebel.'

'Duck down, Sadie,' ordered Isaac, 'It's me that's got the nine lives, remember.'

'I'll join you,' she replied, delving into her bag, 'This is the perfect occasion to try this out. I've had it since Jake first made me the Glove, but I've never had the chance to use it.' Sadie crouched down and spread a bandoleer on the floor - metal spikes were fixed along the length of the leather strip instead of bullets. Then she smoothed down her petticoats, lay down next to Isaac and slotted the end of the bandoleer into a slot in the Glove.

'Where are they? Oh, I see one, two, now three of them. Here goes!' With a squeal of excitement, Sadie sent a hail of darts in the general direction of Double Top's men. A roar of pain showed that at least one of the darts had found its mark. 'Oh, that was fun,' laughed Sadie, a little later. 'I've used them all up now, though. I'll make a dash for the airship, I've got my scooty-bob at the back, so I will be there in a jiffy. Give it a few more minutes, then come and join us. It's time we were leaving,' then she jumped up, adjusted her skirts, climbed over the rail and disappeared. Oliver shook his head, smiling.

'What a girl! Absolutely no fear or remorse about dealing with anyone who threatens the crew. Anyway, perfect timing because these are the last three bullets.'

'Then you should go, I'll hold them off, then follow you.'

'Let me make it clear: we are not retreating; we are escaping!' said Oliver emphatically before leaping over the railing and disappearing from the view of their adversaries.

As Oliver walked briskly back to the airship, he heard a shot. 'That's one,' he thought. Then he saw Sadie standing beneath the airship next to the rope ladder holding her mono-scoot.

'Hello, I thought you would be inside the Rebel by now,' he said.

'Oh, I thought I'd stand guard,' she replied, 'Jake gave me his darts. He may be a brilliant inventor, but he's a useless shot.' Oliver chuckled as he climbed the ladder, hearing another shot from Isaac.

'He's got one more bullet left,' he called to Sadie, then disappeared inside the very crowded gondola.

Sadie heard Isaac's final shot, and a few seconds later, Isaac came running towards the gondola. Then, events happened quickly. Sadie heard a shot ring out; she spun around in the direction of the noise and saw a man approaching from behind a tree. Smoke curled from the musket he was carrying. He stopped to reload his gun.

Sadie realised that he must have crept around through the forest to outflank them. Then she looked back towards Isaac and gasped. He was lying face down, a crimson pool staining the earth beneath his body. Sadie rushed over to him, and he turned his face towards her.

'Ohhh!' Isaac groaned, 'Looks like I must have miscounted those nine lives.' He slumped, and Sadie saw in his eyes that the light had been extinguished. Instinctively, she ran back to get her mono-scoot, then turned to face her enemy.

There had never been a sound like it before. Rosebud reverberated with a rebel yell that pierced the air. Uttering a sound that combined the scream of a cougar with the whoop of a native American, the man began running towards the airship. That cry of fury signified his determination to rid his promised land of all foreigners and protect his birthright. The blood-curdling noise merged with Sadie's primal, bone-chilling scream of rage and anger - a sound that conveyed a hatred of all those who threatened her friends and crew members, together with her seething animosity towards all men who mistreated women. She hurtled towards her target using the scooter's steam boost for the first time, shocked by the speed she was travelling at. Her adversary stopped, aimed, and fired. At the same moment, Sadie flipped off the safety cover mounted on the handlebars and slammed her fist down on the firing button. When the smoke from the musket cleared, only one of them was still alive.

'Sadie!' shouted Oliver, 'We have to leave; our lives and the children's lives are at risk if we stay any longer. Come now!'

CHAPTER TWENTY-ONE

The drawing room in Mrs Bannock's Washington residence exuded elegance and refinement, from its richly patterned damask wallpaper to the fine rosewood furniture and ornate marble fireplace. A maid entered, set down a tray and poured tea for the guests, all except for one who had requested a large tumbler of whisky.

Mrs Bannock took a deep breath. The events of recent years had etched worry lines into her face. It felt like an eternity had passed since that fateful journey in the covered wagon, venturing northward with Jessy and Luke to forge a new life. She looked around at the Rebel Runaways, who were comfortably seated and sipping their drinks. She stood, a faint look of nervousness flitted across her face, and she began to speak.

'I thank you all for coming from the bottom of my heart. Actually, at one time in my life, I would have said this.' She paused for a moment, then slipped into a broad Southern drawl, 'Well, bless your hearts, y'all. I just wanna take a moment to thank each and every one of y'all for coming out today. From the bottom of my heart, it means the world to see all your smiling faces here. We're gathered like this, and it just warms my soul to know we're all here together, supporting one another. So, from me to each of you, thank you kindly.'

Her assembled audience smiled. Sadie clapped her hands softly. Mrs Bannock continued in her normal accent: 'Which is why I wanted to say a few words first of all. I must admit, I'm a little nervous because I've never spoken about this before. You see, everyone I meet takes me at face value. I am the wife of an Army Major caught up in this terrible conflict to save the Union.' For a moment, her voice faltered, but then she caught sight of Charlotte and Sadie, who were nodding their encouragement. 'Our nation is tearing itself apart for many reasons, but the core issue is slavery. I might have shed my accent, but I can't hide from myself that I was born into a household where everyone accepted slavery without question. When I was a little girl, I thought everyone lived on a plantation and had slaves at their beck and call.' Mrs Bannock paused to let the polite ripple of laughter die down. 'I didn't question it. Let me tell you a story. When I was fourteen, we were going on a family picnic, and I wanted to impress some young boy. I had in mind that I wanted to wear my blue dress. Now, maybe I hadn't told the maid, I don't remember, but when she laid my peach dress out on the bed, I was livid. I thought she was being disrespectful. I slapped her across the face and demanded she replace it with my blue dress. She did so without uttering a word.' Mrs Bannock continued, her voice tinged with regret. 'I forever after was ashamed of my actions. Not just because the boy in question took no notice of me.' Once again, her audience laughed, more enthusiastically this time, 'It took me ten years to apologise to that maid. Her name is Jessy, and she is, as you know, no longer a slave but is now a dear friend. So now, before you all, you who were strangers until quite recently, I want to thank you for your bravery and for you to accept my apology for being at one time a small spoke in a hideous wheel that crushed our fellow citizens.'

This time, the applause was louder and more prolonged. Mrs Bannock nodded and smiled in recognition of such a warm response and, relieved, sat down again. Meanwhile, Oliver held out his glass towards the maid waiting at the back of the room. As the maid topped the glass up with whisky, Charlotte couldn't help but notice the track of a tear running down the girl's cheek. Then Oliver reached out, grabbed a spoon from Billy's cup, tapped it on the side of his glass as if to call order, and stood up to speak.

'Mrs. Bannock, allow me to speak on behalf of the Rebel Runaways. I graciously accept your apology, though I must assure you it was unnecessary. Each of us carries a past; it's what unites this eclectic and somewhat motley crew. However, we celebrate the present, and our actions are guided by principles of fairness and justice. You will not realise it, but there is a connection between you and me. It's a cord that stretches across the ocean and occasionally wraps me in darkness and despair. You see, I'm a wealthy man, but my family's fortune was founded on the cotton industry. I needn't expand on the relationship between cotton and the stain of slavery. So sometimes I see the money in my purse as blood money.'

'That's why he's so keen to 'and it over to every bloomin' barman he meets,' quipped Billy, lightening the mood. Oliver acknowledged Billy's remark by raising his glass and taking a sip. Meanwhile, Billy whispered anxiously to Charlotte: 'Bloomin' ain't bleedin' swearin', is it?'

'Tell me about your journey from Savannah,' said Mrs Bannock.

'There wasn't time for grieving for Isaac once we were on the airship because of all the littl'uns,' explained Sadie.

'They had spent most of their lives cooped up in the Rosebud building with nothing ahead of them other than hard labour in the fields, picking tobacco or cotton, and there we were, soaring through the air, crossing America, flying towards safety and a future,' added Charlotte.

'They were so excited, and they loved playing with Billy,' said Jake.

'Well, I never 'ad much of a bleedin' family life. Oops! Pardon my language. Anyways, life was tough as a youngster, and I was pretty much ignored, so I 'ad some playing to catch up with. I tell you, hide 'n seek on an airship's not so bleedin' easy! Oops! Pardon my language.'

'I'm an army wife,' laughed Mrs Bannock. 'I've heard some rich language in my time when the troops thought I was out of earshot.'

'And how is your husband?' asked Oliver, 'I was sorry to hear that he had been captured.'

'He's bearing up. I get letters now and then. He's in Andersonville prison camp in Georgia. He's got plenty of company. There are more than forty-five thousand of our boys in Andersonville. I shan't tell him about poor Luke yet; he will be so upset!'

'We never met Luke,' said Joshua, 'But Isaac often spoke about him. Isaac looked up to him like an older brother.'

'I can't believe how stoically Jessy is taking it. Their relationship was snatched away before it really got going. At least she has a family now that Luke's sister's children are with her.'

'I heard you had set up a kind of orphanage,' remarked Sadie. 'I hope it's not like the poorhouses we have in England!'

'No, it gives them a home. It's for displaced mothers and children and they receive love and support. Those you brought back from Savannah live there, and more are arriving all the time. Jessy is in charge; she's both loving and very practical; perfect for the job,' replied Mrs Bannock.

'It's so hard to accept that Double Top got away with it,' complained Oliver.

'No, he didn't,' asserted Mrs Bannock firmly, 'You hit him where it will have hurt: his coffers. Look at it this way: a fully grown slave is worth around eight hundred dollars, and you brought back twenty-six women and children. That's a substantial sum. When you think that maybe that young girl, June, might have had ten children - there's another eight thousand, plus the other slave girls might have become mothers too in a few years. It's a more lucrative enterprise than growing cotton. Furthermore, consider that he had mortgaged those slaves to the bank to finance the sale of bonds. He'll have to settle that debt somehow.'

'Yeah. If you had killed him, that would have been that, but now it's like stickin' the bleedin' knife in and twistin' it. That's got to flamin' well hurt! 'Scuse language!' said Billy.

'Yes, well, to have landed just one punch on his nose would have been satisfying,' said Oliver ruefully, 'Anyway, we've taken up a lot of your time, Mrs Bannock. Thank you for the refreshments and for all you have done for the children. I think it's time we left these fair shores; I quite fancy a good old pint of ale in an English pub.'

'You can drop Sadie and me off in Paris,' said Charlotte. 'We've got a fashion empire to set up.'

'I've been thinking about inventing some weaponry for the Rebel; I'd like to crack on with that,' said Jake.

'I'd like to see how my charity food stations are gettin' on,' said Billy, 'And I've been finkin' about beans; they would be proper tasty in a tomatoey sauce on a piece of toast.'

'How are your wounds healing, Joshua?' asked Sadie.

'By the time we've flown to England, I'll be right as rain.'

'It's bound to be raining in England,' quipped Sadie

He'll be seein' his sweetheart, Emmy. That'll put a spring in his step!' chirped Billy. Joshua attempted to box his ears, but Billy ducked.

Just then, there was a knock at the door, and a maid announced, 'Excuse me, Ma'am, but there's a lieutenant who says he has something important to tell you.'

'Show him in then.' A nervous young officer entered the room.

'Sorry to disturb you, but I thought you would like to know the news as soon as possible, seeing as you are Major Bannock's wife.' He paused, unwilling to carry on.

'Have you had news of my husband? Is he alright?'

'No, it's not that, it's... it's because of our heavy losses, the difficulty in getting supplies to our troops, and the riots in New York, the Government has decided to call it a day. We've caved in. The Confederacy has declared victory!'

The End

DAVE JOHNSON

A NOTE FROM THE AUTHOR

I hope you have enjoyed my book and will look out for other titles in the 'Rebel Runaways' series.

I want to thank Rachel Laurence for her input into all my books. As an actress, she does fantastic work narrating the audiobooks, but before that, she plays a crucial part in the editing process.

I am also the author of the 'Stuck' series from Amazon. They are stand-alone time travel books suitable for adults and children 8+. You can see them by visiting this page on my website: www.stuckdave.co.uk/blink

You can also join my mailing list and find information about upcoming publications and have the opportunity to win free stuff! I would love it if you followed me on Instagram, too: @stuckdavewrites

I would be extremely grateful if you could write a review of my book on Amazon. Even if you didn't buy this book yourself from Amazon, you could still post a review there.

Printed in Great Britain
by Amazon